You're About to Become a

Privileged Woman.

INTRODUCING
PAGES & PRIVILEGES™

It's our way of thanking you for buying
our books at your favorite retail store.

GET ALL THIS FREE
WITH JUST ONE PROOF OF PURCHASE:

◆ **Hotel Discounts** up
to 60% at home and
abroad ◆ **Travel Service**
- Guaranteed lowest
published airfares
plus 5% cash back

$50 VALUE

on tickets ◆ **$25 Travel Voucher**
◆ **Sensuous Petite Parfumerie** collection

◆ **Insider Tips Letter**
with sneak previews
of upcoming books

*You'll get a FREE personal card, too.
It's your passport to all these benefits– and to
even more great gifts & benefits to come!*

There's no club to join. No purchase commitment. No obligation.

Enrolment Form

☐ *Yes!* I WANT TO BE A *Privileged Woman.*

Enclosed is one *PAGES & PRIVILEGES*™ Proof of Purchase from any Harlequin or Silhouette book currently for sale in stores (Proofs of Purchase are found on the back pages of books) and the store cash register receipt. Please enroll me in *PAGES & PRIVILEGES*™. Send my Welcome Kit and FREE Gifts -- and activate my FREE benefits -- immediately.

More great gifts and benefits to come like these luxurious Truly Lace and L'Effleur gift baskets.

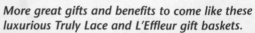

▼ DETACH HERE AND MAIL TODAY! ▶

NAME (please print)
_____

ADDRESS _____ APT. NO _____

CITY _____ STATE _____ ZIP/POSTAL CODE _____

PROOF OF PURCHASE

SAMPLE ONLY

NO CLUB!
NO COMMITMENT!
*Just one purchase brings you great **Free Gifts** and **Benefits!***
(More details in back of this book.)

Please allow 6-8 weeks for delivery. Quantities are limited. We reserve the right to substitute items. Enroll before October 31, 1995 and receive one full year of benefits.

Name of store where this book was purchased_____

Date of purchase_____

Type of store:

☐ Bookstore ☐ Supermarket ☐ Drugstore

☐ Dept. or discount store (e.g. K-Mart or Walmart)

☐ Other (specify)_____

Pages & Privileges ™

Which Harlequin or Silhouette series do you usually read?
_____

Complete and mail with one Proof of Purchase and store receipt to:

U.S.: *PAGES & PRIVILEGES*™, P.O. Box 1960, Danbury, CT 06813-1960

Canada: *PAGES & PRIVILEGES*™, 49-6A The Donway West, P.O. 813, North York, ON M3C 2E8   **PRINTED IN U.S.A**

Sexual combustion

That's what it was, Jake decided grimly as he drove along.

Hollywood made movies about overpowering lust all the time. *Body Heat, Fatal Attraction.* Unfortunately, those stories didn't have much of a happy ending: a man so obsessed by a woman he lost all self-control.

Jake hadn't lost *total* control, although if the passengers hadn't shown up just then... He recalled every taste, every quiver Nora had made.

He checked the mirror for traffic, then angled it so he could see the group. Nora sat by herself, her face flushed, lost in thought. Remembering?

He'd never had a response to a woman like that before. Nora Stevens might not look like a man killer, but her touch made him crazy. He'd wanted to take her to bed on the spot.

Which could blow his cover....

For one memorable summer, **Molly Liholm**—
like her heroine—escorted groups of seniors on
bus tours across North America. Unfortunately,
no one quite like Jake Collins appeared on her
passenger list! Still, she considers not losing
anyone on the weeklong trips an accomplishment.

A Toronto native, Molly worked in publishing
for thirteen years before starting to write herself.
Tempting Jake is her first romance novel. Look
for many more funny, sexy stories from this
talented new author!

TEMPTING JAKE
Molly Liholm

Harlequin Books

TORONTO • NEW YORK • LONDON
AMSTERDAM • PARIS • SYDNEY • HAMBURG
STOCKHOLM • ATHENS • TOKYO • MILAN
MADRID • WARSAW • BUDAPEST • AUCKLAND

For Helen Cherry, Patty Miller and Tiina Vallik, three talented and wonderful women who know more about the bus business than anyone really should!

ISBN 0-373-25652-3

TEMPTING JAKE

Copyright © 1995 by Malle Vallik.

Printed in U.S.A.

1

THE GETAWAY WAS off schedule.

Nora checked her watch again, pretending unconcern. The driver was definitely late. Damn. The plans didn't allow for any delays.

Nora looked down the street, past the groups of milling tourists that seemed to populate every Washington, D.C. thoroughfare, willing the vehicle to turn the corner, to arrive. She double-checked her list. Yes, she was definitely at the west doors of the hotel. According to the schedule, the driver should have pulled up ten minutes ago. She pictured the frustrated driver trapped in one of the city's unending traffic jams, trying to maneuver, cursing because he was *now*—Nora looked at her watch—eleven minutes late. If he didn't get here soon, they'd be caught at the border.

If they got stopped—searched at the U.S.-Canada border—all of her well-thought-out and meticulously researched plans would be useless. That galled her. She hated to fall victim to the unpredictability of others.

To calm her harried nerves, Nora visualized the driver pulling out from behind the truck he'd been trapped behind; he would be just around the corner, now he'd be making the turn.... Damn, still nothing came into sight. She shifted her oversize purse onto her other shoulder and resisted the urge to tap her foot.

A round, normally cheerful-faced man disengaged himself from the small crowd of tourists and walked toward her. He frowned as he looked at his watch. "He's late," Zachary Buch echoed Nora's concern.

Nora waved merrily at a woman with alarmingly red hair who looked questioningly over at Nora and Zachary, then pulled Zachary to the corner of the hotel entrance where they were slightly hidden from the curious tourists. She sighed. Nora hadn't expected Zachary on today's run. She'd planned and worked out the itinerary over many late nights—everything was timed to the last detail. Only now Zachary had turned up. Zachary always thought she needed help. Behind his rotund, positively jovial exterior, Zach was convinced he was hero material and spent much of his time waiting for a crisis to happen so that he could save the day. But the last thing she wanted was for Zach to save her. No, thanks to her, everything was in order...except the driver was late. *Hurry, hurry!* she commanded him mentally.

She smiled her best smile at Zachary, all too aware he wasn't easy to fool. "He'll be here," she said confidently. *Soon*, she pleaded to herself.

Zachary pulled out a well-worn handkerchief and mopped his heated face. "Nora, I don't need to remind you how crucial the timing is. I've calculated all the steps and the margin for error—"

"Still gives us a few minutes," she reassured before Zachary could pull out his calculator and elaborate printouts. She was the one in charge—not him. "I've worked everything out, too. Didn't you always say I was your best student?" she said teasingly but wondered how she had gotten herself involved in all of this.

"*One* of my best students," Zachary corrected. "Jerry Harkness had a lot more promise than you, but he got married and went to work for IBM!"

As Zachary shivered over the horror of leading a conventional life-style, Nora dug into the cavernous depths of her bag and pulled out a bottle of aspirin. For Zachary, working as a peon in a huge corporation was beyond understanding—talk of Jerry Harkness always gave him a headache. Behind Zachary's scholarly facade lurked the soul of an adventurer, one of the last great romantics. That's what had drawn Nora to him and his scheme.

She'd met him through his popular university history course, Great Leaders of the Modern World. Students loved it because Professor Zachary Buch often came dressed as his lecture subjects. Nora knew that he dreamed of doing something great, like the people he lectured about had done. The day he'd worn a toga to class in minus-twenty-degree weather, he'd won Nora's heart. His knees had been far too cute to resist.

He accepted the aspirin, but peered into Nora's purse with hope. "You don't, ahem, have anything stronger in there?"

Zachary's love of overindulgence worried Nora, too. When he was tipsy he became even more loquacious than ordinarily. "You promised me you wouldn't drink until this was over," Nora said. She could see it now—her driver in the hospital after a twenty-car pileup, and Zachary in Betty Ford, regaling all with stories of the fortune he had almost made.

She wasn't about to let that happen! She'd worked too hard and too long. But where was the driver?

Feeling the Washington heat even this early in the day, Nora fiddled with the bow tie at her neck, which was growing as tight as a hangman's noose. With some luck, which was owed her, the weather up north would be cooler, less humid. The polyester of her uniform suffocated her on terribly hot July days. How did people ever get used to wearing these outfits? She never would, but soon she wouldn't have to ever again. Soon her days of watching and saving every penny would be over. If her plan worked.

Why was there never a bus when you needed one?

"Look at that!" Molly Terts poked her friend, then pointed down the street with her well-manicured though wrinkled hand.

Holly Wentworth turned her alarmingly red-haired head to where her longtime best friend was pointing. She kept one foot on her suitcase. It wasn't safe to leave luggage unwatched. She examined the bright pink tube pulling curbside. Even with sunglasses protecting her eyes, the neon colors of the Merry Travelers sign glared mercilessly in the morning light. "I agree it looks rather like a giant tube of lipstick, but you've seen it before."

"Not the bus," hissed Molly. "*Inside* the bus."

Once again Holly turned her attention to the vehicle pulling alongside the Washington Omni Hotel. Despite her sixty-odd years, her eyesight was as sharp as when she and Molly had met as schoolgirls. The sight of the too-pink Merry Travelers bus was a familiar if rather overwhelming one. She scanned the signs covering the bus, checked the tires, saw that all the windows were intact—one never knew in midtown Washington—nothing! The bus drawing to the curb was empty except for the driver— "Oh, my!" Her words were reverent.

Molly nodded. "They never mentioned *that* in the brochure."

"How many bus trips have we taken?"

"At least a dozen," Molly answered without hesitation. She'd spent many early mornings waiting to embark on another Merry Travelers adventure with her energetic friend—usually at Holly's behest. Even during their various marriages—five at the last count, although, as Holly pointed out, there was always hope of upping the number—the best friends would often sneak away from their families. Bus tours were a recent addition. These organized expeditions were short and well-planned, a nice break. The tours were also rife with recent widowers. As a result, the twosome had covered much of the United States and Canada on these activity-filled vacations.

"Perhaps the driver is a new feature. Merry Travelers hasn't put out a brochure in some time. He could be a new marketing angle," Holly suggested wickedly.

"Merry Travelers can't afford to print new brochures because of how much business they've lost lately," money-conscious Molly asserted.

"But if they advertised Mr. Tall, Blond and Beautiful, they'd have buses full of lonely widows and disappointed wives." Holly pulled out a small mirror to reapply her lipstick and check her masses of red curls.

"*I've* never been disappointed. But we're both too old for him by at least—several—years." Molly slanted her hat rakishly over her blond hair.

"He could be what Nora needs."

"*Nora!*"

"Yes, Nora. She's not getting any younger." The two friends turned to consider their tour guide, who was watching the bus with a furious expression on her face. Nora had frequently been their guide over the past five years. "She's a sweet, pretty girl, but have we ever heard her talk about a special man?"

Molly snorted. "She might be sweet to us, but have you seen the deep freeze she gives the Lotharios on the road?"

"My point exactly. Nora has taste. She's not willing to settle for less than she deserves."

"She deserves a bus driver?"

"Yes, maybe . . . Oh, I don't know—" Holly floundered "—but she deserves to have some fun! And if that's not a man who knows how to show a woman a good time, I'll, I'll . . ."

"Pay your son's tuition for business school?"

"Never!" gasped Holly indignantly. "Imagine, I put him in the finest art school, and he wants to make money! I don't know where I went wrong as a mother."

"Perhaps it's his father's influence," Molly suggested mildly.

Immediately Holly calmed down and a soft look came into her eyes. "Yes, poor William, he was an absolutely charming man. He got such a thrill out of playing the stock market."

"And left you very well-off," Molly added. "You can't blame Nicholas or Nora if they're interested in careers."

"Careers!" Holly waved off financial stability with her hand. "It's time Nora stopped working so hard and started playing! Look where that philosophy has gotten me!"

"Riding buses with the over-the-hill gang."

"Living life to the fullest! Always set for a new challenge . . . or intrigue." Holly grinned wickedly. "I predict this will be our best trip, yet. We have our...plans, and maybe we can help Nora."

Molly nodded. "All right, Nora can have the bus driver—if he's good enough. Young people today need to be pushed in the right direction."

"Who'd have thought a bright and attractive girl like Nora would need any help? Why, in our day, you made it your top priority to land a good man and then worried about the rest. Like you and Daniel."

"Or you and Stephan." Holly waved at the man approaching them.

"Yes." Molly sighed with pleasure.

The two friends watched the bubble-gum-pink bus come to a whooshing stop, its billboard claiming: Merry Travelers, We Make Getting There the Fun!

AN APOLOGETIC SACRIFICE—preferably the balding head of her tardy driver—would appease her, *maybe*, Nora decided. After five years of herding groups of travelers through tightly scheduled itineraries, she knew the importance of promptness. If she had a driver who wasn't following the schedule she might as well give up and go home. They'd be lucky to reach the Canadian border before the cross-border shoppers swarmed over the bridge, holding up her bus in their wake. A first day filled with tired, grumbling passengers was not the best way to start their nine-day adventure together. She'd have to stress that *together* part to Bill Wilson, the driver. It was unlike him not to realize how important a good beginning was.

Just three more trips. She muttered her favorite rallying cry. Three more trips, and she could afford to quit. She would never have to follow stupid corporate rules again. And, she continued as she caught sight of her reflection in one of the oversize sight-seeing windows, when she turned in the Merry Travelers uniform, she would never, *ever*, wear pink again. She frowned at the pink, ruffled figure facing her and turned her head slightly to admire the pink suede bow holding back her dark hair. It was carrying the company look to a ridiculous extreme, and that was precisely why she had put it on this morning.

"Are you the escort?"

Mesmerized by her horrid reflection, Nora hadn't heard the driver approach, until his words broke in. And shattered every illusion she had about bus drivers.

Where was her fifty-year-old man with the protruding belly, oily hair and ruddy complexion?

After more bus trips than she could count, from one coast to the other, from short three-day trips to month-long excursions, she had thought she'd met every kind of driver. The bus driver from hell, who, on an especially treacherous mountain road, had asked in a booming voice whether she smelled something burning and then exclaimed that the bus had lost its brakes. He'd then squealed an imitation of a bus barreling downhill, out of control. When they'd finally reached the ferry crossing she'd had to restrain her shaken passengers from throwing the buffoon overboard.

There were the drivers who forgot to plan the route and ended up in Iowa instead of Ohio while Nora tried to amuse passengers who, unlike the man behind the wheel, were able to read road signs.

And then there were the happy-to-be-away-from-the-wife Lotharios, the ones who truly believed that part of an escort's job was to *entertain* the driver, day and night.

This one didn't fall into any category. In front of her stood six feet two inches of raw male animal—there was just no other way to put it, Nora decided, and closed her gaping mouth. His broad chest and muscular arms strained against the confines of the driver's uniform. His face was square and strong and lined. The wind ruffled his blond sun-streaked hair, as he rocked on the balls of his feet, surveying her from head to toe. Studying her polyester A-line, elasticized skirt, her frilly high-necked blouse with its neat bow that matched the offensive one in her hair, and her pink Reeboks! Mortified, Nora saw herself in his eyes—hidden by reflective aviator glasses, naturally—and knew she looked like a "before" picture in a makeover.

Gathering what little dignity she could, she said, "Be grateful they don't make you wear pink,"

"You have a point there. Pink has never been one of my better colors." She could hear the amusement in his voice, but saw no accompanying smile. When she continued to bemusedly stare at him, he asked, "You are the tour escort, Nora Stevens?"

"Tour *coordinator*," Nora corrected automatically. *Escort* had too many connotations—although with him they might be worth exploring. His voice was low and raspy, the kind a woman dreamed of hearing from the pillow next to her. She was still stunned by him, so her mouth took over and expressed the thought that had been concerning her for the past fifteen minutes: "You're late."

"I'm the new driver, Jake Collins," he answered smoothly. "There was an accident—"

"You need to plan for eventualities like that. Here—" Nora pulled a map book from her purse and opened it at one of the highlighted pages "—these are some excellent alternative routes when traffic is jammed. If you listen to the traffic reports on WBBK from five to six-thirty and then switch to WBBC when Jess Whitman begins his reports, you'll have the Washington roads covered. This—" Nora had found the other item she wanted and thrust it into the driver's hand "—is a list of the best radio traffic reports throughout the U.S." Nora dug around some more in the cavernous depths of her bag. "Bruce must have kept my Canadian lists! He knew I wanted them back! Never mind, I'll have him fax them to us at the hotel tonight." Nora suddenly recalled the reason for the delay. "Was anyone hurt?"

Jake's head was bent over the papers. He straightened slowly and was looking at her but she still couldn't tell what he thought because of the annoying aviator glasses. "What? Oh, the accident. Only a fender bender, but it backed up traffic for blocks."

Glad to hear there had been no injuries, Nora smiled at him, but mentally berated herself. Her need to organize, to ensure events ran efficiently had the consequence of occasionally irritating some people. At least that was how her mother would phrase it. Nora could admit, when she was being completely honest with herself, that she was just plain bossy.

With the experienced glance of a single woman, she checked the driver for a wedding ring. There wasn't one. She did a quick mental scan of her suitcase, selecting her most attractive outfit for tomorrow. Luckily, just as all the pink signs covering the charter bus could be removed, tour escorts—*tour coordinators*—only had to wear the Nightmare in Pink on the first day of a trip. At least she had an easier time than the male escorts.

"It won't happen again." Jake's voice was cool.

Nora couldn't tell whether he was annoyed by her behavior or he considered her a minor nuisance. Irked that she should elicit no response from the man, she took a deep breath and brushed a nervous hand against the hairs tingling at the back of her neck. She'd worked too long and too hard to have her plans upset now. Three more trips, and she'd have the money she needed.

She couldn't see past the reflection of the aviator glasses but knew Jake was studying her. "I'm looking forward to working closely with you," he said, breaking the silence. "The other drivers said you were the . . . best."

The hairs on the back of her neck stood up. Good heavens, she chided herself, that was what she got from giving her libido too little exercise. Or was it guilt, her conscience demanded, because Bruce Davis, the owner of Merry Travelers, suspected . . . ? No, Bruce wasn't a problem. Nora pushed aside her worries, reminding herself that her ability to remain calm in the face of disaster was legendary among the other tour coordinators. Why, she'd found the only one-hour photo-developing shop in the wilds of British Columbia when an entire busload of Japanese visitors had wanted to develop their film *immediately* because one of them believed he'd captured Bigfoot on film; she'd walked up the steps of the Empire State building with a group of fitness fanatics; she'd mediated when Molly and Holly had set their sights on the same man; and she'd thrown a block that would have made an NFL player proud when a Finnish couple had decided they needed to conceive their first child at the Statue of Liberty!

One... unusual bus driver was nothing she couldn't handle. Her neck tingled in answer. She didn't have time for a man now! Tomorrow, she'd wear a different hairstyle, one that didn't expose her neck. "Are you a new driver?" she asked, to get her mind back on business.

"Replacement. The scheduled driver is sick, I was called last minute. Weren't you notified?"

No smile softened his face. Nora wondered how he was going to enjoy living with rambunctious passengers for the next nine days. Then the meaning of his words sank in. "No. I... no." The bus company always notified her about a change in drivers, no matter how last-minute. Nora quelled her rising unease, telling herself everything was in place. As long as the new driver knew how to drive, she could handle the rest. In fact, that was how she preferred it.

Nora swung her bag off her shoulder, and Jake jumped out of its way. "Sorry," she mumbled as she rummaged through its contents. "Here—" she handed Jake a pile of papers "—I've outlined the best route and the cleanest washrooms for stops and the times in between. Although—" Nora consulted her watch "— we're—"

"Late," Jake supplied. "I won't let it happen again, boss." For a second, she thought he was going to salute. Instead, he looked at the documents Nora had given him. "I thought planning the route was my job."

"Of course it is, Mr. Collins," Nora explained patiently, used to this reaction. Drivers could be very territorial about their jobs, but once a driver began to use her system, he always agreed it worked the best. Sure, she'd had a few failures, a couple of drivers who requested not to work with her, but then, not everyone was as particular as she was. "But I've been over this route many times and am more experienced. I just want our passengers to have the best trip possible. If you follow my suggestions, I'm sure you'll find everything clearly marked, and you won't have any extra work to do."

"Just follow your instructions?"

"Yes, that would be best for everyone," Nora agreed.

What looked like a grimace passed over Jake Collins's face, although it was gone so quickly, it was hard to be sure. Then he spoke in a conciliatory tone that made the hairs on Nora's arms prickle. "Okay, boss. I'll load the luggage, you handle the passengers."

She nodded, giving him her best tour-guide smile, glad that she'd established the fact she'd be in charge, pulled the seat-assignment list out of her multicolored tote and began boarding the passengers. After moments of organized activity, Nora had her twelve passengers settled, their large quantities of hand luggage stored overhead, and Jake was steering the bus away from the hotel. *Just three more trips*, Nora repeated to herself as she picked up the microphone to begin her enthusiastic "you're-going-to-have-a-wonderful-trip" speech.

Out of the corner of her eye, she saw a speeding car begin to move into their lane. She gasped as Jake slammed on the brakes, avoiding the vehicle. Nora tried to catch the pole in front of her too late and landed facedown in the bus aisle. She spat out a piece of dirt, pushed herself up and glared at Jake.

"Sorry about that . . . boss," Jake said. Nora saw the twitch of a smile on his lips.

Rubbing dirt from her polyester A-line skirt, Nora looked up to see her twelve passengers struggling against their smiles and silently chanted *Just three more*—when the bus swerved again and Nora dived for the pole. This time she caught it, but she knew, just as the captain of the *Titanic* must have known, the last thing she'd be having was a wonderful trip.

2

Welcome to the wonderful world of Merry Travelers! Adventure, entertainment and the opportunity to learn all—at a reasonable price! On Day One, we leave Washington for our good neighbor, Canada. Settle back in our luxurious motor coach—the most advanced form of bus travel, with all the modern conveniences, including bathroom, driven by an experienced professional—and enjoy the scenic journey and commentary of our professional escort as we travel across the longest undefended border in the world.

JAKE CHECKED his mirrors and pulled the bus into the fast lane, ignoring Nora's glare. Let little Miss Priss have a dose of excitement in her life.

He couldn't believe he was driving a bus full of senior citizens. When had his life come to this? And the bus wasn't even full; it was more like a scattering of the soon-to-be-dearly-departed. This was going to be one hell of an assignment. He'd thought Miss Merry Sunshine was going to have heart failure when he'd examined the bus from front to back after all the passengers had boarded. She'd kept pointing at her watch, so he'd moved even slower.

But he hadn't found anything suspicious, so the deal had to be going down later. Maybe at the border.

Hell, with any luck, he could wrap up the investigation before the day was out. He wasn't looking forward to spending any more time with the tottering nursing home escapees or anal-retentive tour escort than he had to. For fun, Nora probably wore knee-highs instead of panty hose. He shuddered. And her breathless gasp when she'd corrected the escort-coordinator stuff. He'd known what she was thinking.

Never. Ever.

He had a job to do and then he was the hell out of here.

"GOOD MORNING, EVERYONE. First, let me make sure no one onboard thinks this is the Number 3A to downtown Washington. No? Good, because we're off on nine action-filled days through Toronto, Montreal, Quebec City, and one night in Gaspé, Quebec.

"Now, here's the route we're taking...." Nora held up a map on which she had highlighted their route and passed it around. The simple act of showing passengers the direction they would be traveling pleased them immensely—and made for better tips.

"Next, I'll be passing out the name badges that I ask you to wear for at least the first couple of days. I count the number of passengers onboard, but until I get to know you, I might pick up a wrong person!" As the group laughed at her oft-repeated joke, Nora realized she wouldn't be having that problem on this trip—the twelve faces were all familiar. Once again she was going to be spending her days and nights with a group whose average age was triple her own. The unfortunate part was that her merry seniors often acted younger than herself.

Molly Terts and Holly Wentworth—the Traveling Terrors, as they were affectionately dubbed by Nora and her co-workers—had been on this trip with her only two weeks ago.

So had Stephan Papas. Nora suspected that one of the two was interested in the charming, elderly Greek gentleman, but as the two women were always together, it was hard to know who was after whom.

The foursome from the Happy Days Seniors Home was also traveling together again—Janet Rule, Alicia Hall, Ben Riley and Harold Anderson. The group whiled away the hours playing cards—anytime, anywhere. They were setting up a game as Nora spoke.

John and Tim Chance—quiet, almost-secretive brothers—were next. She knew that John was a widower and Tim had never married, but not much else. They had been on her New Orleans Mardi Gras excursion, doggedly following Molly and Holly like lovesick puppies. The dozen was completed by Mr. and Mrs. Reid, a couple who had recently sold their small variety store and retired. Zachary Buch was sitting across from them, busy striking up a friendship.

Nora and her friends in the travel business often referred to Merry Travelers as Merry Widows and Widowers because of its popularity with the senior set. Bus travel appealed to retirees because of the leisurely pace and economical rates. During the height of the season, coaches were filled with Europeans who'd eagerly come to America to visit relatives, but after a few weeks, were more eager to escape them by taking a bus trip. In September, this business dropped off and the seniors returned.

Still, Nora always felt comfortable in these groups. She had been a shy child, unable to even gain much attention in her large family, until her parents, in desperation, had suggested she become a camp counselor one summer. Nora had dreaded the prospect, but had agreed because she always agreed. To her surprise, she'd been an extremely good counselor, because she didn't have to be herself. She had a position, a role to play, and that's what she did. That was also how she had ended up riding buses with the silver set.

She genuinely liked older people because they were past judging everyone on superficial matters like looks and position. Nora's college friends—those who had managed to find *careers* not jobs—thought her choice of occupation lacked prestige, but she had ambitious plans. And she liked working with people who had some time to talk, time to enjoy the world around them.

But this bus trip was beginning to become really weird. While it was usual to have familiar faces among her passengers, it was unusual to have them repeat the same trip. As one of her favorite little old ladies had said, if you're only on this planet for one trip, why take the same road twice?

It was also unusual to run a bus with only a dozen paying clients. This group was smaller than family dinners at Nora's parents. The trip wouldn't make Bruce Davis, the owner of Merry Travelers, any money.

It was even more unusual to have a driver like Jake Collins.

Neck hairs on alert, she could feel his eyes on her as she made her way down the aisle handing out name tags. She should be thrilled to have this chiseled paragon of manhood trapped with her for nine days, but her annoying little voice was saying that something—everything—was just too unusual. *Only three more trips...*

She wished she could be more like her friend Sandra who would seize an opportunity like this. But men like Jake Collins made Nora nervous because she was too susceptible to them. One look had confirmed it. Jake had charm, sex appeal and a natural way with people. One wink of his eye, one flash of a killer smile and he'd get whatever and whomever he wanted. Nora sighed. No matter how hard she worked at being gregarious, it just didn't come naturally to her. And when she was confronted with a type like Jake Collins, well...

She always fell for them.

Not that the guys always knew that she was...*smitten* was the word she liked. The old-fashionedness of the term suited her relationships. In kindergarten she had been best friends with Wayne, the funniest guy in the class. It had remained that way until high school when she realized that she was falling for a type. While she dated the sensible boys, the practical boys who were attracted to her quiet personality, it was the devil-may-care, bring-life-to-the-room boys she secretly lusted for.

After she'd worked hard to become less socially inept, to actually enjoy life, she'd even managed to date Frank Jeffries, the captain of the football team. But Frank discovered a mousy library-sciences student who inspired him with a passion that Nora could only dream about. They eloped right after he won the big game.

That had been a hard lesson, especially since Frank and the mousy librarian were still together.

So she'd returned to the safe, responsible boys, but they continued to bore her.

Then she'd gone after a couple of the reckless, adventurous, oh-so-sexy guys, trying to find another Frank who'd want to settle down with her this time, but Harrison and John had both dumped her. With her pride hurt more than her heart, Nora had thrown all her energies into her work—and it was about to pay off!

Now, her love life consisted of pleasant flirtations with the men she met on the road.

Jake could never be a nice, pleasant flirtation.

Nora realized that Holly was talking to her. "What?" She needed to start concentrating more on what was happening instead of making up imaginary problems, Nora reminded herself sternly. Molly and Holly were among Nora's favorite passengers; their zest for life appealing—although Nora hoped that she wouldn't be traveling on bus tours at their age.

No, she'd prefer drinking champagne on the French Riviera with her much younger lover. Even more, she'd prefer visiting the grandkids, but her success so far made the first image seem like a stronger possibility. Maybe when she hit her sixties she'd learn how to be wild.

Still, so many of her friends had husbands, that she hated to be left out. But she shuddered to think of all the difficulties involved in teaching a man—especially the kind that she really wanted—the proper routines. Her life was well organized. Too organized, according to her friends. While Nora had to acknowledge that she had stuck to her plans rigidly, she had succeeded. Once this job was over, though, she'd see if she couldn't fit a prospective love interest in somewhere.

Maybe Molly and Holly did have the right idea.

"I said," Holly repeated, "we want your address so we can write to you from Egypt."

"We're spending the winter on an archaeological dig," Molly added cheerfully. "I've always been interested in history. Mummies and curses are *so* romantic! My second husband promised me a dig for our honeymoon. When he took me to Acapulco instead, I knew the marriage was doomed!" She offered Nora her much-thumbed address book and as Nora wrote, she continued, "What happened to Bill Wilson?"

"Yes, dear, I'm sure Bill was supposed to be our driver on this trip—at least that's what Bruce said when we signed up." Holly's brown eyes twinkled. "Although Mr. Collins is certainly pleasant scenery."

"He is, isn't he?" Nora stopped herself. Bill Wilson was one of the regular drivers Merry Travelers used, and Holly's comments reminded her that if he had signed up for a tour it would take a natural catastrophe to keep him away.

Holly patted Nora's hand reassuringly. "But where did you find him? He's nothing like our regular drivers!"

That was exactly the question that had been nagging at Nora, but she wasn't about to worry the ladies. She was more interested in why Holly and Molly were on the Montreal-Quebec tour again. "I was so pleased to see you this morning. We just did this trip two weeks ago. I thought you didn't like to repeat the same trip."

"Normally we wouldn't, but we had some...business that we left incomplete last time. And you know me, I can never pass up a bargain."

"Free is some bargain," Molly agreed.

"Free?"

"Well, yes." Holly looked at Nora questioningly. "Didn't you know? Bruce said that we were such loyal customers and as this tour would be running half empty he gave it to us as a gift."

Nora tried to mask her surprise. In her three years of working for Bruce Davis he had never given anything away—he didn't like throwing out the garbage. Feeling too much like the hapless Gopher on "The Love Boat" for her liking—would her boat analogies never stop?—she finished writing her address and moved on to the Happy Days gang.

"I believe our Nora finds Mr. Collins very attractive," Molly divulged after Nora had left.

"How can you tell? They've only spoken a few words."

"You always have the same look in your eyes when you see a man you're interested in."

"Really, Molly! How do I look?"

"Intrigued, eager, alive—like you did when you met Daniel."

The friends smiled in memory of their shared secret.

"Do you think Mr. Collins is as intrigued by our Nora?"

Molly considered for a moment. "I don't know...and you know how men are fooled by bad packaging."

The two stared at the broad shoulders of their new driver. Molly poked her friend. "Look, he's staring at us in the mirror!" They smiled as Jake hunched down in his seat.

Holly patted her curls. "Nora needs to be pushed in the right direction, and we're perfect for the job."

"Two busybodies who like to meddle?"

"Well put. As I said, this should be a very interesting trip."

JANET RULE DISCARDED a card, pulled at her hand-knit sweater—which had metallic goldfish hanging from the trim, Nora realized—and smiled at her. "We were pleased to see that you would be our escort this trip." The white-haired woman put down her hand as if she was out of luck and then announced, "Gin." As her playing companions grumbled about her luck with the cards, Janet reached for her white vinyl purse. "Did you see the photos of my grandson's first birthday?"

"You showed her the whole scrapbook last time. Leave the poor girl alone," Ben Riley interrupted, trying to stretch his large frame in the cramped space. The cardplayers had immediately commandeered the seats that swiveled to face each other—elbowing Holly and Molly out of the way to get them. "Do you think we'll be across the border before six?"

Nora enjoyed the foursome, even though she was constantly barraged with endless pictures of their grandchildren. Janet and Alicia Hall spent most of their time shopping for presents for their grandkids. Ben was always obsessed with time, fiddling with the watch on his massive wrist, checking another timepiece in his breast pocket.

"Only if the traffic is good and there isn't a long lineup at customs," she answered.

"Relax, Benjamin." Alicia dealt the cards, her voice quelling. "You'll have lots of time to run your errands. We're looking forward to a nice, relaxing trip." Alicia frightened Nora just a little, with her no-nonsense ways, her gray hair pulled back into a severe bun, her skirts tweed even on the hottest summer days, her shoes always practical. Sometimes Nora worried that she was staring at her own future.

"Yes, of course. I'll just be taking it easy." Ben smiled at Nora. He and Janet usually paired off together, but Nora wasn't sure if that was because of mutual interest or just to get away from the overbearing Alicia Hall. Harold, who was more a part of the background than anything else, meekly asked for two cards, and play continued.

Three more trips, Nora muttered to herself.

"PENNSYLVANIA IS well known for its vast amounts of coal and for something much closer to my heart, Hershey's chocolate. Named after the town of Hershey— or was the town named after the chocolate?—the air is filled with its delicious aroma."

As her passengers oohed their delight, Nora continued with her talk on the state of Pennsylvania. "In 1680, Quaker William Penn petitioned for land in the New World for a Quaker colony—"

A sudden sharp turn had Nora stumbling and landing heavily against Jake. She let out an "oomph," resting momentarily against his solid presence. "That's the third time," she warned.

"You should be more careful. It takes skill to keep your balance in a moving vehicle," Jake said, not taking his eyes off the road.

His calm ruffled Nora. "I've been doing everything in a moving vehicle for the past five years without any problems until now. You drive as if you're in a high-speed chase rather than a leisurely tour," she complained in a low voice so that the passengers couldn't overhear.

"You've done *everything* on a bus?" Jake's words shivered along Nora's spine. "Maybe you can teach me a thing or two."

She ignored what her overactive imagination immediately offered. "What I can teach you is how a driver should behave," she snapped more curtly than she'd meant. Taking another deep breath to calm her too-quick temper, she glanced down the long aisle of the bus to see if any of the passengers had noticed their argument. Most were busy reading the magazines she'd passed out earlier, the Happy Days foursome was still involved in their card game. Zachary was typing into his notebook computer and then scowling at his watch. Molly winked at Nora. She turned back to Jake, determined to get answers to the questions that were bothering her. "What happened to Bill Wilson?"

"He called in with a flu bug or something."

Nora recalled that the Merry Travelers office was short staffed; maybe someone had forgotten to inform her of the switch. It hadn't happened before but it was possible. She tried a different approach. "I'm surprised we haven't met before. I know most of the drivers—"

"I'm pretty new. How long have you been doing this?"

"Five years."

"And you've been with Merry Travelers the whole time?"

"Yes, straight out of college. I did some part-time work while I was in school—" Nora stopped. She was supposed to be questioning him.

"Something wrong?" Jake turned to look at her but his glasses still hid his expression. Nora wondered if that hard face ever smiled. He continued smoothly, "Sorry about that spill earlier. It won't happen again, boss."

"If we're going to work together, you'd better call me Nora." And then she added guiltily, "And you're right, I'm not your boss. We work as a team."

He moved his head to take another look at her in surprise. She smiled at him. "Come on, the other drivers must have told you I'm the bossiest guide there is, but that's only because I want everything to work according to schedule. I, *we*, pack a lot of traveling into a few days, and—"

"I understand . . . Nora. I promise to look over your material." Jake's voice became much warmer, inviting. "Since I'm new at this you'll have to fill me in on what's expected on one of these tours. For example, what was in all those bags I put underneath the bus for you?"

Nora's stomach sank to the floor in dread. "Haven't you played bus bingo before?"

"It looks like you're going to be opening up new horizons for me, Nora."

She definitely didn't like this. Anyone who had been on a bus for more than two days had been subjected to bus bingo. Unless . . . "How long have you been doing tours?"

"About three hours."

"This is your first trip?" Nora couldn't keep the incredulous note out of her voice. Her bad feelings were giving birth to anxiety. Maybe Bruce Davis did know about her plans and had sent Jake Collins to investigate— No, that was impossible!

"This is my first time driving a bus. Fast cars are more my style."

"But we never get inexperienced drivers." Nora didn't understand. It was customary for drivers to have years of experience before they had enough seniority to qualify for a Merry Travelers charter tour. How had a new driver managed it?

Tours were fought over by senior drivers because they broke up the routine of doing the same line-run over and over again. And tours paid well and could pay off again in tips. A seven-day excursion got a driver away from his family—an added bonus for a man during his midlife crisis.

"Maybe a computer error got me here, and maybe poor Bill," Jake continued, "is reporting to fly a 747."

"Stranger things have happened." Nora retreated to her seat in the front row, ignoring Zachary who was trying to subtly catch her attention. Her anxiety was now tying itself into complicated knots throughout her body. Out of the corner of her eye she saw Jake glance at her but she continued to stare straight ahead at the Appalachians.

She knew all of her passengers so that would make her job easier, she argued. And she would just ignore how wide Jake's shoulders were and the way the back of his hair curled over the top of his collar. Until she knew why he was really here, she could fantasize but she couldn't touch. Her future was on the line. If something went wrong now...

But her normal sense of optimism and humor returned. She wouldn't fail. This trip was odd but, she smiled to herself, she'd dump Gopher as a role model and figure out how cruise director Julie would have handled the situation.

No matter how hard she tried, though, she couldn't fit Jake Collins into the paternal role of Captain Stubing.

3

After our full day of travel to Toronto, Canada—no, there's no snow in July—enjoy a relaxed night's sleep in our superior hotel. If you have the energy, trendy Yorkville offers dining and clubs. For those of you who want to be refreshed for a full day's sight-seeing tomorrow, experience the comforts of room service.

"WHERE ARE THEY ALL?" Jake demanded. How in the world had twelve cane-toting, peppermint-sucking old people gotten away from him?

Nora took a deep breath and turned what he was beginning to realize was her Let's-pacify-the-crazy-person's-request-no-matter-what expression toward him. But then she glared at him and moved to rip his sunglasses off his face. Instinctively, he grabbed her wrist and held her frozen, slightly off-balance. Her wrist felt small and fragile under his strong fingers. Just as he thought she was going to fall against him, she raised her other hand to push away from him. "I can't see what you're thinking when you wear those things." She motioned furiously at his glasses.

Surprised that irritated her, Jake remained silent. Nora didn't. "I told you not to let them off the bus!"

"The redheaded one said she only wanted to get a cup of coffee." Jake couldn't believe they'd tricked him like that. He'd opened the bus door and the next thing he knew, they'd all disappeared.

Nora reached back and unclipped the big pink thing holding back her hair and massaged her temples. Her hair was nice and shiny, he noticed. "That's Holly. You really are new to this business aren't you? In Niagara Falls, home of every tacky tourist souvenir ever invented, you let our merry travelers loose." She sat down on the bus step; Jake continued to stand in the deserted parking lot in front of the Holiday Inn. Nora had asked him to pull over once they crossed the border so that she could phone the office and have them fax her the information she wanted for the next day. As she'd exited the bus she'd insisted he not let anyone off. But he hadn't listened. By the time he'd returned from the hotel lobby where he'd made his own phone calls, the bus was deserted.

"I'm sorry," he said. He was, too. Who knew what his gang of elderly escapees was up to? This case was proving more complicated than he'd imagined.

Nora shrugged. "How were you to know?"

"What do we do now?" he asked.

"Wait. We wait," she replied wearily. "Sooner or later our happy shoppers will return, most likely when the stores close. In the meantime," she suggested with the spark Jake was getting used to, "this might be a good opportunity for you to go over the schedules."

Jake thought it might be, too.

EXHAUSTED, NORA DROPPED onto her bed and relaxed. After ten hours on the road, not including the delay in Niagara Falls, they had finally arrived in Toronto. She had settled the passengers with strict instructions to assemble in the lobby at 8:45 a.m. for their city tour.

No doubt the merry revelers were busy making entertainment plans among themselves.

All she wanted to do was to take a hot bath and go to bed.

Unfortunately she couldn't. She had arrangements to make.

Quickly, Nora cleaned up and pulled out her white dress. Peter, the assistant hotel manager, liked sexy, and she wasn't above using a few feminine wiles. With any luck, it wouldn't be too long before she was in bed—without Peter.

At the knock on the door she checked her watch but Peter wasn't due for another twenty minutes. Wrapping her robe more tightly around her and touching the back of her neck, she opened her door.

If Jake Collins had managed to look good in the poorly cut driver's uniform, now he looked dangerously wonderful in jeans, T-shirt and black leather jacket. No points for imagination, but a ten for effect.

"Getting ready for bed?" he all but drawled, the emphasis on the last word creating all kinds of seductive pictures in her annoyingly overactive imagination.

"No. That is, I'm getting changed." She was pleased her voice was so even despite her racing pulse. Steady,

Nora, she told herself. This man was not for her. He'd only lead to trouble. But oh, what trouble!

"Good." He stepped inside her room and surveyed it. "I thought we might have a drink while you tell me more about my duties."

The room shrank. Her open suitcase, with her pink teddy on top, was drawing his eyes like a flashing red— pink—light. He smiled wickedly, and Nora thought of the moment when his hand had held hers. "Pink does seem to be your color," he said.

Nora snapped shut the lid of the offending valise. "I'm busy tonight."

"Busy? You have a date?"

Hot with embarrassment, Nora flared. "You needn't sound so amazed—and yes, I have a date." Softening her tone, she offered an alternative. "I'll meet you to-morrow morning before our tour." She should be grateful to have a driver who was so interested in his job . . . if that was really what he was interested in. She still wasn't convinced Bruce Davis hadn't sent Jake Collins to spy on her.

Jake crossed his arms and stared at her. Now that he wasn't wearing his glasses Nora saw his eyes were hard, like steel. "Seven-thirty in the coffee shop," he agreed.

"I'll be there," Nora promised.

Jake didn't move. Instead he continued to look around the room, making Nora more and more ner-vous. *Three more trips*, she reminded herself. She was definitely letting her guilty conscience get the best of her. Jake Collins might not look or act like a regular bus driver, but that didn't mean he wasn't. That didn't mean Bruce Davis knew....

Wasn't it just her luck to finally meet an attractive man who was practically her captive for nine days when she didn't have time for him? Unfortunately, she always had to make her own luck. Jake Collins—no matter how attractive, no matter that he looked at her with pure male interest, no matter that she couldn't remember her last date—could not interfere.

Or could he?

As she was weighing the pros and cons, Jake interrupted. "Who is this sight-seeing guide meeting us tomorrow? Don't you do the tours?"

Nora tugged the belt tighter around her, discreetly checking whether any stray bits of flesh were left exposed. *Just three more trips.* "It's against the rules. In each city we're allowed to tour on our own bus, but we have to use a guide licensed by that city's tourist board."

When Jake still made no move to leave despite her dismissive tone, Nora walked to the door and opened it. "Tomorrow," she said firmly.

Jake took his cue. "Tomorrow." But it sounded more like a threat than a promise.

HOURS LATER JAKE STOOD in the dimly lit Bamboo Club on Toronto's trendy Queen Street West sipping a beer. He'd been surprised by Nora Stevens tonight. Jake wasn't often surprised.

At first, he'd thought it only too natural that she filled her days and nights by traveling with a bunch of old fuddy-duddies, she fit in perfectly. Her body was trim and her skin unwrinkled, her hair shone a rich brown without a speck of gray, but her attitude made it clear that she was only waiting for time to correct its mistake, so she could fit in physically with the over-the-hill set.

They were welcome to her. With her dark hair pulled back tightly, the buttoned-up-to-forever blouse and sensible shoes, she was not his idea of a merry traveling companion.

Playing nursemaid to a bunch of geriatric vagabonds wasn't his idea of a merry vacation, either, but it was necessary if he was going to get the job done. He was good at getting the job done, at doing whatever was necessary. He'd dismissed Nora as any danger to his hormones, but now he was having to revise his opinion. Not that it would have mattered if she looked like Kim Basinger; he liked a good time, but sex never interfered with his work.

Still, he had to wonder why an attractive woman like Nora hid among a group of has-beens. He'd listened to her throughout the drive. She liked those people but she kept a tight rein on herself. He'd seen genuine flashes of amusement but her laughter was always restrained. Her walk was controlled; no sudden moves. Hell, she was one controlled woman.

Except when she'd tried to take off his glasses. The memory made him smile.

He had the feeling her sudden change in appearance tonight wasn't the real Nora Stevens letting loose, but a means to an end. Was she planning to seduce the hotel guy? Why? The guy was okay-looking, but Jake knew Nora could do better—namely himself. At least that's what his female acquaintances assured him.

Not that Nora's date would interfere with his investigation. What could interfere were those two excitable old biddies who'd eyed him like he was a prime slab of beef. Jake had caught one of them checking him out while he was driving. He was used to female admiration, but not from women who'd grown up in another century. Considering that the average age of his companions was a hundred and two, his biggest task might be keeping all of them alive.

The case should be a cinch to crack; he definitely wasn't dealing with the criminal minds of the century. And he wouldn't have to worry about keeping up with the arthritic seniors. Jake scowled; he'd given up working these small cases long ago. If it wasn't for E.J., he wouldn't be doing it now.

Here he was, Jake Collins, one of the best undercover operatives the U.S. Customs department had, and he wasn't even one hundred percent sure the beating that had put E.J. in the hospital was related to the case. Jake swallowed some beer, remembering all the equipment hooked up to her, the quiet faces of the nurses, how bruised and pale and still E.J. had looked. He blamed himself because he hadn't really listened to E.J.'s theories about what was happening at Merry Travelers; his own work had been so much more challenging.

He'd only worked with E.J. a couple of times, but they'd worked well together. And, he'd admitted reluctantly, he liked her. She was funny and honest and more than willing to point out when he was being pigheaded.

Two days ago in the hospital room when she'd finally opened her eyes, he'd felt that terrible pressure binding his chest release and known he must check out this two-bit bus operation.

The problem was, U.S. Customs didn't know what was being smuggled aboard the Merry Travelers' buses. They just knew something was. The tip-off had come from a small-time criminal bargaining any information he had to lower his charges. His claim had been unusual enough to warrant further investigation and had turned up a very puzzling series of circumstances. Ever since Bruce Davis had taken control of his mother's company it had lost money, but Davis's life-style had become more and more extravagant. His personal bank account had received regular deposits of twenty thousand a month. Too good for a charter bus tour operator.

The investigation into Bruce Davis had also uncovered some unsavory friends; in particular, companions he shared with Angelo Lucci. Lucci's syndicate, which controlled most of the Eastern States, was involved in everything from drugs to gambling. It wasn't enough to convict Davis of anything, but it was suspicious.

Jake's gut told him Davis was guilty, and he always trusted his instincts. Not that he didn't do the research and check out the leads—he smiled, thinking of Nora's elaborate notes and schedules—but it was his instincts that made his case record the best in the department.

And the key to whatever was going on with Davis and Lucci was the buses crossing the border. Simply seizing a bus wasn't enough. With Lucci's luck, Customs would stop a bus with nothing on it but outraged tourists. No, they needed to know what was going on before setting the trap.

E.J. had joined the Merry Travelers head office in D.C. as an office temp and found one connecting pattern: The tours all spent at least five weekdays, *business* days, in Canada. She had determined that the trip Jake was on now had to be a smuggling run.

All he had to do was keep his eyes open and wait for the exchange. End of story. It was almost too easy. He frowned. Nothing was ever that easy.

He drained his glass and watched Nora on the crowded dance floor. She was wearing a short, clingy white thing that revealed a very different woman from the efficient and sexless tour guide. It had taken little effort to learn that her date was the assistant manager of their hotel.

Jake was tired of the smoke in the club and waved a hand, trying to clear his eyes. He discovered a redhead at the end of the cigarette that was clouding his vision.

"Sorry," she said. "I'll put it out." She smiled.

The redhead looked good and had nice teeth. He was sorry he didn't have the time, but Nora and Peter were leaving. "Another time," Jake said with regret and followed them. This assignment definitely wasn't going to be any fun.

Whatever Nora and Peter were discussing captivated the two so that Jake didn't need any particular skill to avoid being seen as they walked along Queen Street to the hotel and then through the lobby. Jake raced the stairs to Nora's floor, the fifth, beating the elevator. He turned the corner ahead of them, stopped and peered back around. Nora and Peter had stopped at her door. The dirtbag didn't even unlock her door for her, Jake noted sourly. She held out her hand. "We're agreed, then?"

Peter looked at her hand as if he had a better way of closing the deal, but shook it and then watched her shut her door in his face. He raised his hand to knock on the barrier, but let his hand fall before he could act out his thoughts. Coward, Jake thought as he went back to his own room.

So they weren't lovers. He was surprised, again. He didn't like surprises. Jake pulled out the list of passengers' bedrooms he'd charmed out of the front-desk clerk. He'd noticed the Reids in the hotel coffee shop. He would search their rooms first.

What the hell was going on here? What was Nora up to? Why had the old fogies given him the slip just after the border crossing?

As he worked the lock on the Reids' door, Jake decided that even more than surprises he hated bus tours.

NORA MADE HER bleary-eyed way to the coffee shop. At twenty-eight, she was getting too old to stay up half the night and then expect to put in a full day. *Only three more trips . . .* But she managed just a small portion of her usual enthusiasm. Coffee would make her feel better.

Jake was already there, drinking the coffee she craved and eating a breakfast she could barely look at. He saw her and waved to a waitress. As Nora put her bag on the extra chair and sat down, the young woman hurried over. Nora croaked, "Coffee."

"Late night?"

Nora refused to respond until she had drunk most of her first cup and indicated a refill. "No food." The waitress left with a last lingering look at Jake.

"Not a morning person." His tone remained bland although Nora knew there was *something* behind his words.

And why was she contemptuous of the waitress's admiration for Jake when her own thoughts were no better? Despite the fact that Peter was charming and attractive, last night her mind had strayed too often to Jake Collins. Once, she'd even thought she'd caught a glimpse of his broad leather-clad shoulders, but the figure had disappeared before she could get closer. And her undisciplined imagination had also pictured him lurking in the hotel hallways. She needed to stop working so much.

Maybe she should have accepted Peter's unspoken invitation last night. She'd known him for several years; he was a decent guy and interested in her. Her rule about not getting involved with co-workers left her no one to get involved with. If she'd spent the night with Peter she certainly wouldn't have dreamed about Jake and his shoulders and what it would be like to run her nails across them. What it would have been like to kiss those firm, wicked lips. How Jake could have taken what he wanted, what she wanted.... Oh! She felt the heat rise in her face as she remembered her dreams about them and buried her face in her coffee cup, hoping he wouldn't see the sudden blush.

Even in the crowded coffee shop Jake was different. Even wearing the neatly pressed uniform he didn't look like a man who made his living driving a bus.

"Why are you on this tour?" As usual, the words were out before she could stop them.

Jake finished his eggs and pushed the empty plate away. Now that he'd had a chance to meet some of his fellow drivers staying at the hotel, he was beginning to realize why everyone was so surprised by him. He was way too young—maybe he could convince Nora that buses were in his blood, that instead of police hats and shiny badges, he'd received model buses and atlases as Christmas presents. That he'd played bus driver in the basement instead of good guys and bad guys. And he definitely needed to practice smiling. "What do you mean?"

"You are not the kind of man, Jake Collins, who suits shepherding groups of happy vacationers," Nora insisted.

He shrugged. "I'm just a man who needs a job." He leaned back against the vinyl cushions. At least they were a damned sight more comfortable than the bus seats. Maybe that was why drivers packed on the pounds. "What should I be doing?"

"Well, here you two are! I told you, Holly, that Jake and Nora would make a good team." Molly Terts, her blue eyes alight with mischief, beamed happily.

Her companion nodded. "Yes, you did. Now let's get our breakfast and leave them alone." Holly grabbed Molly by the arm.

"But I wanted to know what they were..." The words trailed off as one friend dragged the other away.

"Are those two what I should expect for the next thirty years or so?" Jake asked, as the two women settled at a table at the other end of the coffee shop. Molly waved at him. He was unsure how to respond so he tried a smile. Molly looked confused.

"More or less," Nora agreed. "The best thing about this business is the people. It's also the worst thing. You meet the most unusual types."

"Like your date last night?" While going through rooms, Jake had puzzled over what arrangement she and Peter had made. Had Peter "arranged" for the goods to be put on board the bus? If so, the team Jake had arranged to search the bus today while the Merry Travelers were sight-seeing would find them.

"That was business." Nora shifted uncomfortably under Jake's skeptical gaze. Why did he look so doubting? It was past time to reassert her control over their relationship. "Today we've got a full-day city tour and then the cocktail party in my room."

"Party?"

"It's a Merry Travelers custom, and a chance for the passengers to meet and mingle in a more relaxed setting. I hold the party in my room so the company doesn't have to pick up an expensive bar bill."

"Toronto is a very dry city on a Sunday. Where do you intend to buy your liquor?"

"I brought it with me."

"Across the border?"

"Of course." At Jake's questioning look she continued, "Buses are never stopped at the U.S.-Canada border, so we're notorious for smuggling."

"You're never stopped?" Jake kept his tone even but wondered what he was dealing with. The case couldn't be this easy! Maybe Nora was trying to throw him off track; after all, she was on more of these trips than any of the passengers.

"Hardly ever. But before you decide to bring back a new sound system you'd better check out the prices north of the forty-ninth parallel. I doubt if you'll find it worth the gamble."

"Have you *ever* been stopped?"

"Once, in five years." Now that the coffee was kicking in Nora felt better and she smiled at him benevolently. "Not bad, hey? If you want to know the secret hiding places on the bus, just ask—I've got some good ones."

"I'll bet."

Nora was surprised at how hard Jake's voice was.

He stood. "Let's go and collect our merry old coots."

"They're not old coots, they're . . . free spirits."

"Whatever you say," Jake replied, clearly not believing a word. "I looked over your route and you're wrong. There's a better turnoff after Exit 67."

"Oh, no, we've tried it before and it took longer."

"According to all the maps, it is definitely the shorter way," Jake insisted and walked out.

Nora stared after him for a second, then took off in pursuit. Of all the nerve! What did he know about planning bus routes? *Just three more trips . . .*

HOLLY NUDGED MOLLY as she watched the pair leave together. "See how tired they both looked? Maybe the romance has already begun!"

"Your hair dye is seeping into your brain cells. Nora isn't the type of girl to fall into bed with a man on their first date. If she was, she'd have a man in every bus station . . . like you."

"Humph, you're jealous because I have Daniel. Besides, I'm sure Jake and Nora just went on a nice date and then lost track of time."

"I don't think so." Leaning forward confidentially, Molly lowered her voice dramatically. "I thought I saw Jake spying on me in the hallway at four this morning!"

"Spying?" Holly frowned. "And what were *you* doing in the hallway at four this morning?"

When Molly only smiled, Holly exclaimed, "You sly little thing! Let's go make our . . . arrangements while Jake is with Nora, and you can tell me all about last night."

"I'm not the kind of woman who kisses and tells," Molly said with a giggle, "but you can tell me which dress you think makes me look sexier—the blue or the green?"

"Definitely the blue."

4

Every Merry Travelers trip offers exciting opportunities to dispose of your income—we're talking shopping. Outlet malls, high-class galleries, ethnic marketplaces. Don't forget to leave some empty space in your suitcase for your shopping bargains!

JAKE'S BRAIN HURT.

All that cheerfulness from Walter, the tour guide, and the eager questions from the merry old coots had him wishing for the nice solitude of a stakeout.

While he'd parked the bus the galloping seniors had escaped, as had Nora with Walter. To make another "arrangement"? he wondered sourly.

He'd had to wait by the bus for everyone to return.

Jake hated waiting. At least on a stakeout he was expecting something to happen, but on this "easy case" he didn't know what he was waiting for.

He hated easy cases.

In his twelve years of experience—he'd been recruited by the government straight out of college—the little cases had too often proved the most dangerous because of their unpredictability.

When he'd spent four months tracking the stolen Montclair jewels, he'd been part of a well-equipped team who knew they were tracking professionals. Professionals who would use violence only as a last resort. It was the amateurs who were unpredictable.

He tried to stretch a kink out of his back—that damn seat was uncomfortable. Maybe he spent too much of his time behind a desk these days, searching through psychological profiles and computer printouts on statistical trends. Even when he was out in the field, he was usually the team leader, coordinating his operatives. This was the first time he'd been undercover in almost two years. Jake grimaced when he realized how long it had been. He wouldn't even be here now if the case hadn't been personal. Still, when he got back to D.C. headquarters, he'd ask for a transfer to a unit where he could have more hands-on involvement. Hell, he'd been with the D.C. branch for almost four years. He'd never stayed any place that long before. He must be getting old.

Out of the crowd of tourists he spotted Nora and Walter walking back toward the pink bus. Jake was beginning to hate pink as much as Nora did. Worse, Nora and Walter were not returning from the museum but from the opposite direction. Where had they been?

"Have a pleasant lunch?" Jake asked when they arrived at the bus. Walter straightened his multicolored cartoon-character tie and pushed the wire-rimmed glasses back up the bridge of his perfect nose as he turned a smile filled with perfect teeth on Jake.

Nora flinched under Jake's cold words. Walter Hanson, the step-on guide, had taken the group through a dizzying tour of Toronto, along the Lakeshore to Harbourfront, the New and Old city halls and the Royal Ontario Museum.

Jake had wanted to join her and Walter for lunch, but Nora had managed a quick exit through a staff door at the museum. Other than the fact that she couldn't imagine impeccably groomed, gossip-loving Walter entertaining Jake, she'd wanted to finalize her plans with the guide. She turned guiltily toward Jake. Maybe a life of skulduggery wasn't for her; she felt like the employee with her hand caught in the till. Or maybe Jake really was too curious about everything.

"Yes," she answered brightly. "Walter never stops talking. We got caught up on all of our colleagues." She stressed the last word, wanting to create the impression that it was only a gossip-filled lunch.

Walter beamed and puffed up. "Nora is a great girl. You should be glad for the chance to work with her before—"

The sudden weight of Nora's purse on Walter's foot stopped him midsentence. She faced him apologetically. "Oh, I'm so sorry, are you hurt?"

"No, it's nothing," Walter gasped, hopping on one foot, examining his shoe for scuff marks. Nora glared at him until he finally realized she wanted him to be quiet. He then claimed a pressing need to be elsewhere and hobbled off.

Jake retrieved the colorful bag and handed it back to Nora reluctantly. She never let it out of her sight. "What do you carry in there? Walter will be lucky to escape with only a few fractured toes."

Instantly contrite—her purse was large and it had taken years for her to develop the upper body strength needed to carry it all day long—she asked, "Do you think he'll be all right?"

"Walter is the kind to always survive—he's so smooth most everything probably slides off him." Jake was surprised to find the man had annoyed him. What did it matter who Nora spent her time with? If she had a thing for a male clotheshorse, that was her bad taste.

"Walter annoyed you?" Nora was shocked that anyone could disturb the ever-cool Jake Collins.

"The man never shuts up."

"Agreed, but he is popular with the passengers."

"And as a luncheon companion?"

"His stories about who's sleeping with who are fun, but I always worry about what he tells the other tour people about me."

"Then why have lunch with him?"

"He's useful," she answered, then frowned.

Jake pushed further. What was she up to? Surely she couldn't really be attracted to Walter? "You seem to spend a lot of time with men who are useful—your date last night, Walter..."

"When you've been in this business longer you'll realize the importance of maintaining goodwill."

"Even when you don't like them?"

"Was I that obvious?"

"I'm good at reading people."

"Jake, on this tour you and I *are* Merry Travelers," Nora said with conviction. "We have to make sure everything runs smoothly and maintain good relations for the next tour. Although," she added with a giggle, "annoying Walter wouldn't upset anyone too much."

"Yes, boss." He'd have someone check out Walter as soon as the search team finished with the bus. Canada Customs was aware of his investigation and had agreed to provide a team to search the vehicle this afternoon. If he was lucky, he might be able to wrap up the case before the day was out. But he didn't expect it.

Puzzled by Jake's response, Nora waved her group onto the bus. Remaining on the steps, she picked up the mike as Jake checked his mirrors to pull the vehicle into traffic. She grabbed a pole to hold on to. "Normally, after the museum we'd drive to Chinatown because it was one of the few shopping districts in Toronto that remained open on a Sunday. But as the government has declared Sunday shopping legal." She paused dramatically as all the women snapped to attention. "How many of you would rather shop at the Eaton Centre?" At the unanimous show of hands, Nora told Jake, "We can go south to Dundas—"

"We're not going to Chinatown?" He'd studied the maps and found an excellent shortcut to the drop-off. Nora was wrecking all his plans.

"Why, no. If our *paying* customers prefer to do something different, we try to accommodate them. And the first rule of bus travel is, given any opportunity, our passengers want to shop."

Jake scowled, put the bus in gear and drove along the crowded streets to the mall. Nora was too busy reciting the current Canadian exchange rate to puzzle over why Jake was so concerned with the change in plans.

But after having deposited the happy shoppers, when she saw Jake standing next to a tree under the glass-roofed galleria, Nora hurried over, determined to find out. "Do you ever smile?" she demanded. She knew he did; she'd seen him charm several female hotel employees and she'd seen him flirt briefly with Molly. So what was wrong with *her*?

Somehow Jake's lips flattened into an even straighter line. "What do you mean?"

"In the last—" Nora consulted her watch "—thirty-six hours, I have not seen you once look like you're having a good time." The fact that he was so determinedly uninterested in her more than piqued her ego. She was the only female under sixty on the bus. Jake's behavior was positively disheartening.

"I make my own amusement." She could just imagine!

"Oh, never mind." She grabbed his arm and pulled him along—and not because she wanted to touch him, she assured herself. "You look as out of place here as at one of Molly and Holly's tea parties." At a peculiar noise from Jake, Nora shot him a quick look but he wore his usual nonexpression.

"I'm not fond of malls," Jake agreed placidly.

"How do you buy your clothes—or do you let your girlfriends choose?" She couldn't imagine Jake letting someone else control his life.

"Mail order."

"I should have known. Come on, let's go back to the bus."

"The bus?" Jake stopped midstride.

"I'm tired of the crowds. It'll be quiet there."

Jake took her elbow and began to steer a path through the hordes of shoppers. "Good idea, but let me buy you a drink. We can sit in some comfortable chairs and talk."

Nora halted at the front of the bar Jake was practically dragging her into. "No. I want to go to the bus— I left my briefcase on board and I have some files to finish." When he didn't move, she said, "You don't have to come with me. Just give me the keys and tell me where you parked the bus." She would have liked the opportunity, though, to get a few answers to her questions.

Jake ran a hand through his hair. "Never mind, I'll take you." He looked desperately around the mall.

"Here—" Nora turned and pointed, wishing he didn't sound so annoyed at the prospect of being alone with her "—that's the door we came in from. Orientating myself in these shopping meccas always gives me trouble, too."

As she led the way outside sharing her tips on how to remember the "you are here" in any given shopping maze, Jake considered his options. His men had only had the bus for half an hour; they wouldn't be finished searching for at least another two—well under the allotted shopping time. He'd originally had the arrangements set up for Chinatown, but Nora had thrown those plans for a loop. Now this!

Out on the street, she asked, "Which way?"

"This way," he answered and began to walk east. He went past the first stoplight, the fast-food restaurants and discount shops, but at the second intersection he slowed and pretended to carefully examine the street. "Over there," he pointed south to a street where several buses were parked and began again. At the next corner, he stopped. "I'll be damned."

"What is it?" Nora gasped as she caught up to his long strides. She looked around and then considered him. "You've lost the bus, haven't you?"

"Not lost," Jake hedged. "Misplaced, maybe."

"That's okay," Nora reassured. "I've heard of this happening before. We'll stop a policeman—"

"And report a missing bus? I'd rather find it myself than be the laughingstock of the Toronto police force." Jake had to admit Nora took his cowardice with good grace—she laughed at him.

"You lost a five-ton bus!"

Several polite Torontonians gave Nora a wide berth as they walked past and stared. Jake shrugged uncomfortably. "Nora—"

"This is better than losing my virginity, at least it's a lot more original!" Nora couldn't believe those words had escaped her mouth. Ever since she'd met Jake she'd been thinking about sex far too much.

Jake thankfully didn't comment but looked around at the Torontonians who were still studiously ignoring them. "Do you have a form for this? An NGLBOFD? New guy loses bus on first day?"

"It's your second day."

"You mean I also lost the record?"

Nora collapsed against a railing. She'd bought his ridiculous story but she didn't have to be so amused by it. When she recovered, they agreed to split the area around the Eaton Centre and search separately. Jake wandered the streets slowly, enjoying the mix of people on the streets. In a souvenir shop he found a T-shirt with a female Royal Canadian Mounted Police Officer and the slogan The Mounties Always Get Their Man, which he bought for E.J. After an hour, he headed to the large underground parking lot the Canadian officials had told him about, where the search team was finishing with the bus. Carl Withers, the team leader, came up to him, wiping his filthy hands on his shirt. "Nothing," he reported.

Well, Jake hadn't really expected the investigation to be that simple. Instead, he drove the bus to the pickup spot on Dundas Street, where Nora was waiting. Relief showed on her face.

"Thank goodness!" she said, climbing onboard. "Our merry travelers should be here in about twenty minutes."

She looked pretty today and was smiling nicely at him. She was full of contrasts, easy to be with yet incredibly secretive. What was she up to? He gave her his best smile but she hardly seemed to notice as she sat in her front seat and opened her briefcase. Not wanting to face her elaborate schedules, and a little too curious about all the men she was spending her time with, he asked, "So how did you?"

"How did I what?" Nora asked.

"Lose your virginity?"

Nora looked like she didn't want to tell him, but then as if realizing she had opened the topic, she said, "Summer camp. He swam all the way across the lake— took him three nights. The first two he was too tired...." She blushed. Nora knew she shouldn't ask, but couldn't help herself. "How about you?"

"Baby-sitting."

"The baby-sitter seduced you?"

"No, I was baby-sitting *her* kids."

"Oh."

Jake enjoyed having Nora speechless. "And trust me, I have lots of stamina." He doubted Walter could claim that.

Nora buried her head in her file; she knew that Jake was still watching her, his eyes gleaming with mischief. What was she doing flirting with him? She knew better, much better, she reminded herself.

Jake was exactly the kind of man she could fall for. The result would be nothing but trouble.

Didn't she deserve a little fun? her libido demanded. No! She quashed her desires. They were only together for a few days—after that, Jake would be looking for the next conquest, charming and smiling at the next woman.

She had to finalize her plans for her future. A good-looking, sexy man had no part in it.

For the first time, her future didn't look so great.

"THE DOMED STADIUM was my favorite," Stephan Papas asserted. He smiled affectionately at Molly. "There's a game tomorrow evening. Perhaps you would care to join me?"

"Stephan, are you flirting with me?" She batted her eyelashes.

The old-world gentleman would have twirled his mustache, if he had one, Nora decided. "We Greeks know the art of love and you, my dear lovely lady in blue, deserve to be treated to the best."

Nora surveyed her party with satisfaction. The twelve passengers and Jake were spread out on the two double beds and the few hotel chairs passing plates of junk food around. Not exactly the Ritz, but the travelers always enjoyed the chance to get to know one another better. Somehow, a party held in a small hotel room always had a bonding effect. Tonight she had very little work to do. Her guests were mingling freely because of how well they knew each other. Molly and Stephan were performing the steps of a dance very familiar to them while Holly entertained the Chance brothers.

Mrs. Reid, her wig slightly askew, had cornered Jake at the makeshift bar, in reality the desk, and was regaling him with tales of her health. "My doctor says I'm only allowed one drink a day," she rasped, holding out her oversize glass. "Fill it up."

Jake accepted the elderly woman's flirtation. He raised his eyes to Nora and she tingled. Jake returned his attentions to Mrs. Reid.

Damn. Nora rubbed her neck. After his words this afternoon she hadn't been able to say anything—and she was not what she considered a woman of few words. Luckily the Chance brothers had arrived.

Stamina indeed! Nora pulled her errant thoughts back to the party when Zachary Buch made his way over in what he believed was his unobtrusive manner. She still didn't know why he'd felt it necessary to be on scene.

"I wish you had told me you'd be taking this trip. I could have planned for you," she whispered irately. The round man beamed at her. Zachary Buch looked like a snowman. His circular face was outlined by a ring of hair surrounding the top of his bald head. Years of sitting behind a desk had accumulated in a beach-ball stomach. The perfect embodiment of a jolly, fat man, the image was belied only by the determination that he sometimes allowed to show in his eyes.

"I thought it best to keep my activities quiet. A man has to be careful. Are all of our plans in place?"

"Yes." She wished he wouldn't grill her at inopportune times. She was still surprised that they were involved together, that Zach had volunteered to finance her plans.

"Good. We'll get rich yet, Nora, my dear. I'm very pleased. I know I can depend on you."

"Depend on Nora for what, Mr. Buch?" Jake's hand on her shoulder startled her almost as much as his question.

"Why, I depend on Nora and *you* to make my trip a pleasant one," he answered smoothly. "But if you'll excuse me, it's late and I have an early start tomorrow."

With a cheerful wave to all, Zachary left the room. As if this was the signal for the end of the party, the remaining guests began to make their exit. Jake and Nora were soon the only two left. In a few minutes they'd thrown out the disposable glasses, packed away the surplus chips and straightened the furniture. "A drink?" Jake asked as he opened a beer.

"Why not? A beer," she agreed as Jake poured her one into a glass and sat down on the floor next to her, leaning against the bed.

"You're good at this," Jake began. "Everyone warms up to you quickly."

"It's easy on this trip—everyone's a repeat customer. No matter how charming I like to think I am," she added, "you can't please everyone. I had a passenger once who'd only eat tuna-fish sandwiches with rutabaga. The tuna was easy enough, except when we stopped at a fancy French restaurant and the chef

wouldn't dream of making anything so demeaning as
a tuna-fish sandwich. We compromised on a fresh sea-
food crepe that included tuna. I asked the man to
imagine he was eating an especially runny tuna-fish
sandwich."

"What about the rutabaga?"

"Still haven't the faintest idea what it might look like.
Some things are beyond the call of duty."

"But you still love this job. I'm not sure I could do it
day after day."

"After growing up as one of five kids, it takes a lot to
try my patience. And, I suppose," she admitted, "it's
still part of my desire to be noticed. At first I thought
getting a doctorate would make me stand out from the
rest of my family, then I discovered that my talents at
mediation and entertainment—I always tried so hard
with my family—work in this job." Nora loved her
family but they drove her crazy. Her parents had both
worked, her father putting in lots of overtime to pay the
bills and to put the five kids into university. As the eldest, she'd been responsible. She'd enjoyed being in
charge, knowing whose doctor's appointment the sec-
retary had phoned about, the dates of school recitals
and football games, and remembering to order the
birthday cakes, including her own. Those skills were
easily transferable to her present job and would be even
more useful when she ran her own tour company.

Because she made so many mistakes in her own life—
always choosing the wrong man—she liked organizing
other people's. And she liked trying to figure out what

the secret to long-lasting relationships was from couples celebrating their lifetimes together. She was sure there was one.

Moreover, she was frustrated by the way Bruce Davis was running Merry Travelers. He was missing a lot of good opportunities because he didn't understand the pleasures of bus travel. She did, and she planned to do better than any other tour company with her own business.

As long as Zachary didn't talk too much. As long as Jake Collins was simply a bus driver and not some kind of spy sent by Bruce Davis.

"The passengers like you. Especially Mrs. Reid," Nora added.

"I think that's because I'm not like the usual drivers they have along on their trips. Anyone under the age of forty-five is a novelty."

"You noticed, did you?" Nora smiled at him and for the first time, he smiled back. It was warm and wonderful and would have knocked Nora off her feet if she'd been standing. It was a good thing this guy doled out his smiles sparingly; otherwise Holly and Molly would soon be fighting over Jake!

Since he'd broached the topic of how . . . unusual he was—as a bus driver—Nora opened her mouth to ask some personal questions, when she stopped cold. Jake was looking at her—in a way that froze her motor functions.

"When I saw you yesterday, I thought you fit the over-the-hill set perfectly," he said in his midnight-rich voice, moving close to her.

"And now?" she gasped.

"I was completely wrong. You're a very attractive woman, one I'd like to get to know a lot better." She watched his lips come closer. *He really is going to kiss me!* was Nora's last thought for some time. She felt odd, like she was hurtling somewhere she'd never been before; she wanted to get there but was afraid at the same time. Then her own hands were wrapped around Jake's shoulders, pulling him to her, exploring his muscular strength, and Jake was kissing her ear. That felt good, too, and gave her a chance to breathe—okay, pant. His tongue was lightly stroking her tender lobe and the base of her spine tingled. Nora had never known those two parts of her body were so directly connected.

"How are you going to get rich?" Jake's voice was soft and warm as if he were whispering words of love, and it took a moment for the words floating around her brain to register. The effect could only have been equaled by the entire bunch of the Merry Travelers suddenly bursting out from her closet.

She struggled out of his arms and stood, still panting. "How dare you?" she demanded.

"Nora, what the hell is wrong? We were just kissing." Jake stood and moved toward her.

She backed up. "Oh, no, you don't. I'm used to being kissed because a man wants to, not because he wants information."

Jake had miscalculated badly. He'd planned a little seduction. He'd meant to surprise her. The problem was that *he* was the one who'd been surprised—again. Nora packed a wallop in her kisses.

She had to be part of the smuggling ring—whatever it was. E.J.'s records had showed that Nora had been the guide more often than the others. But what the hell was going on? His team had found nothing on the bus. He was searching the passengers' luggage, room by room, but so far had discovered nothing. Unfortunately several members of the tour carried large bags with them at all times. Tim Chance kept a backpack with him, Nora had her humongous tote, and Alicia Hall carried a paisley bag from which she constantly pulled out cards and knitting.

But one of his suspects must be picking up the goods on a business day and smuggling it back to the States. What he needed was some evidence so he could get backup. It wasn't easy tracking twelve busy tourists, but U.S. Customs didn't want to waste any more manpower on this assignment. Jake figured if he could stick with Nora, she could unknowingly help him investigate the others. In a day or two he'd receive the background information on the tipsy revelers.

And as for the kiss, it had been good, but not overpowering. He was sure other women had felt as good in his arms as Nora. Or close to it.

"Sorry, Nora. I didn't mean anything by it. I just overheard you and Zachary talking."

She took a menacing step toward him. "Do you always ask such questions while you're kissing a woman?"

"Not always." Jake couldn't resist the grin. "I guess I just didn't keep my mind on what I was doing."

Only his years of training got him out the door ahead of the ice bucket.

5

Who wants to spend their vacation time asking directions and consulting road maps? Leave your worries behind and join in the fun of a Merry Travelers tour! You'll meet new friends and discover new places.

NORA SPAT the water out of her mouth wishing it was Jake's face and not the porcelain sink at the receiving end. How dare he! One minute he was kissing her senseless, the next he was asking her senseless questions.

Jake Collins had kissed her for information.

Unfortunately she had liked it.

Nora stared at her empty bed, another reminder of how foolish she had almost been, and knew she wouldn't be getting any sleep soon. Grabbing her purse, she headed out.

She wandered up the brightly lit but mostly deserted Yonge Street. Toronto's most infamous street—and the longest street in the world, her ever-present tour-guide self reminded her—was quiet. Only a few of the homeless and street kids were out. Nora liked the quiet garishness of the Yonge strip. The faded paint and loud posters offering sex shows grounded her in reality. She had to remember there was a hard side to even this safe city.

She had made a mistake tonight. She wouldn't do it again.

Maybe all Jake had been doing was making a pass at her. He was an extremely attractive man and probably used to women falling all over him. Just like she'd been doing. His question had probably been from curiosity, not because Bruce Davis knew anything....

The plans for her own tour company were in place. As long as Zachary managed to remain discreet and she closed the last deal, she'd have made it. Freedom, independence and financial security would all be hers.

The idea that Bruce Davis had sent Jake to spy on her was absurd. But then why was Jake sticking to her like glue? It had taken fancy footwork to drop him today. And his question about Zachary was very suspicious....

And he was a really good kisser.

Telling herself the first thing she would find herself—after closing the deal—was a boyfriend, she returned to the hotel. *Just three more trips*, she whispered to herself as she inserted her key into the lock of her hotel-room door. A soft giggle interrupted her and she turned to see a very feminine robe disappear into Mr. Papas's room. Nora was pleased that *someone* was having some romantic success.

Then she sensed him.

Slowly she turned her head. No, there was no one in the corridor. Still, she couldn't shake the feeling that someone had been watching her. She walked the few steps to the fork in the hallway. There was no one to the right, but she heard a door click on the left. Spinning, she headed that way, mentally checking off room numbers. The Chance brothers' room was down here. She stopped in front of their door, put her ear to the panel and listened.

"Miss Stevens, can we help you?" a voice behind her asked. Nora whirled to face Tim Chance. His small frame quivered with indignation, much like a furious mouse. His nose twitched and his eyes went pink.

"Why are you peeking through our keyhole?" John, the larger, more imposing of the pair, demanded.

"Now, boys," Holly interrupted from behind them. "I'm sure Nora just didn't want to disturb you." She fixed Nora with such a determined stare that Nora could only nod. "We've had a perfectly lovely evening on the town but now I must go to bed."

"Wait—" Tim reached out and held on to Nora just as Holly started to drag her off. "What did you wish to see us about, Miss Stevens?"

John had moved, too, effectively cutting off the determined escapees.

"Oh, er, nothing. That is . . . I was checking to see whether or not you wanted to come on our walking tour tomorrow. Holly and Molly and I," Nora added, inspired.

John beamed at Holly. "Yes, that would be very pleasant—"

"We can't," Tim said, cutting him off. Despite his size, he was the leader of the two.

John straightened. "Of course, I forgot our... appointment. Have a pleasant day." Pointedly, he stepped away and the two watched as Nora and Holly retreated around the corner.

Everyone was acting very oddly, herself included, Nora was forced to admit. Back at her door, she asked, "Have you ever had one of those days, Holly?"

The older woman patted her on the shoulder. "Honey, I've had years like that!"

ON THE LEDGE, outside the Chance brothers' room, Jake edged along toward the window he'd left open in the hallway. He slid in and then pressed himself close against the wall, hidden by heavy dark curtains. He heard Holly Wentworth leave and grimaced.

This assignment was just too weird.

His thorough search of Tim's and John's possessions had revealed nothing except an inordinate fondness for sports: They owned football jerseys, baseball caps, jock-endorsed underwear, leisure suits designed by Tommy Lasorda and more athletic shoes than a department store—everything except a jockstrap. Tim and John Chance were embodiments of the couch-potato athlete.

Deciding to cut down on his own TV sports viewing, Jake realized Nora must have somehow caught a glimpse of him and chased him down to the Chance brothers' bedroom. He'd like to have seen their outraged expressions when they caught Nora peeking in through the keyhole. He caught himself smiling and stopped. It wouldn't do to be distracted, but he'd never chased such a bunch of kooks before!

AFTER TWO SUCCESSFUL meetings and several hours spent shopping with Holly, Molly and Alicia Hall, Nora felt much better and went off for dinner to meet the world with a smile. Everyone had dropped a ton of money and Alicia had had to stop twice at a bank to cash travelers' checks. Nora followed the maître d' to her table.

Jake Collins was already there.

Her cheerful smile froze and then faded. Jake scowled as he rose. Nora seated herself and flipped open the menu. He watched her study it, furiously ignoring him. He'd spent a fruitless day following Janet Rule and Harold Anderson. They'd sneaked out of the hotel guiltily but Jake had quickly realized that was because they had dumped their overbearing companions. They'd met no one, only taken a walk and had lunch.

Jake broke the tense silence. "After you've memorized the menu, you'll have to look at me."

"No, I don't." She closed the menu she had been using as a shield between them. "I'm perfectly capable of eating in silence. And of informing the restaurants that we don't wish to be seated together. In fact, I can do that right now." Jake had learned that it was customary for restaurants to seat tour guides and drivers together— to give them a chance to get away from the passengers.

As she picked up her bag and rose, Jake grabbed her wrist, holding her still. "No, wait, Nora. I'm sorry about what happened last night. I behaved stupidly and I'd like the chance to begin again." Nora was still his best bet for figuring out what was going on. Besides, seducing her would be the one good thing to come out of this assignment.

"I'd like to forget last night ever happened!"

"I can't forget what it was like to kiss you, Nora."

"Jake . . ." This time he let her pull her hand away.

"I'd like for us to be friends. Please, stay."

His eyes appealed to her and Nora weakened. "I'll agree only if we keep our relationship strictly professional. No more repeats of last night."

"Agreed."

Nora settled her tote back on its own seat and ordered dinner, wishing she didn't feel disappointed that he had acquiesced so readily.

"Last night, you said something about doing a doctorate. What happened?" Jake inquired, looking hopefully at her.

Nora debated whether or not to accept his olive branch. Jake seemed to be genuinely apologetic, and she prided herself on creating good working relationships with all of her drivers. And she could never stay mad for longer than twenty-four hours. Besides, she wanted to know a lot more about him. The best way to get information was to reveal some about yourself.

"I was a bright and eager philosophy major finishing my masters at Georgetown University and facing a career in airless rooms with dusty books. But one day I looked out the window at the sun and realized I wanted something different. I quit that same day. Because I had languages as a minor, Spanish and French and a little German, and because Washington is such a tourist town, I got a part-time job doing step-on tours. After my family and my days as a camp counselor, the job was a natural. I did a lot of work for Merry Travelers and when Bruce Davis needed another full-time coordinator, I applied. That was five years ago.

"Bruce Davis?"

"Yes. Actually, his mother hired me. She began the company but Bruce took control three years ago and has expanded the business phenomenally. He's managed to sign on a lot of European carriers."

"Davis does well with Merry Travelers?"

"Yes, very well, although—"

"Although it's unusual to run a bus with only twelve passengers," Jake finished for her.

Nora was glad for the opportunity to discuss her nagging worries. Did this mean Jake shared them, or was he trying to lull her into a false sense of security? Oh, what a tangled web, she concluded glumly and sighed. "I've been with this company for a long time and Mrs. Davis would never have run these half-full tours. In the past few months I've been on several. So have the other escorts. These tours shouldn't be running."

"Why are they?"

The answer to this annoying question had kept her tossing and turning until the early hours on more than one occasion, and its possible answer—the formation of a competing company, hers—had her flushing guiltily.

"Nora, you do know something. What is it?"

"Sometimes I'm worried," she answered softly, "that maybe Bruce is running these trips to make sure a competitor can't cut into his market." She waved her hand airily. "It could be anyone." *Including herself.* Was she forcing Bruce to behave in this irrational manner?

Jake considered her words. Was she trying to throw him off track? "Possible." He looked around the restaurant and caught Holly's eye. She gave him the thumbs-up sign. "Those two approve of me—or rather of us." He waved at the two.

Nora shifted. "They've been trying to marry me off for years. They mean well but thankfully they're harmless—I'm still single." Picking up a saltshaker and studying it, she said, "You're not what we usually get on these tours, so Holly and Molly have naturally picked you as husband material. Do you have a 'significant other'—" she guiltily remembered last night's kiss "—back home?"

"I've just moved to Washington so I haven't met all that many people, women, yet. And no," he said, "I didn't leave a wife behind. I'm not the marrying kind." For once he spoke the truth. If he could avoid his mother's matchmaking efforts for years, escaping the clutches of Holly and Molly and their plans for Nora and himself would be easy.

Then again, this case was supposed to be easy. He'd better watch himself. . . .

Normally, he avoided women like Nora; women who wanted to plan family schedules and vacations, who worried about nutrition and good dental plans; women his mother thought were perfect for her darling boy. No one who worked with Jake would have believed that three or four times a year Jake gave in to his mother and went out an a blind date. It was easier than constantly saying no. But the women bored him. After one date when he tried to be as pleasant as possible, he never called them again. His mother accepted his decision and then spent months trying to find a better candidate.

His mother would probably pick Nora.

Nora didn't bore him, because every once in a while he caught her looking as if she were imagining him and her making torrid love. None of the other sensible women ever had that look.

Maybe there was a wild Nora just waiting to be unleashed. Jake smiled, imagining Nora greeting him at the door after a hard day at the office, dressed in an apron and pearls and nothing else.

She must have understood his look because a flustered Nora grabbed her purse. "I bought something for you today." She foraged through the bag's contents for a minute and pulled out a small sack.

Jake took it and pulled out a black marker and a notepad. Nora looked at him expectantly.

"It's for black marks—every time I get too bossy, you mark one down."

"And how many are too many?"

"Good question." Nora laughed. "No one's figured that out, yet. My record is thirty-three."

"How does it work as a deterrent, then?" Jake teased.

"I'm an overachiever. I hate black marks. Give me my tally in the morning, and I promise to do better. And I am sorry for being so rude to you the first day."

Nora's sincerity made Jake uncomfortable. He was determined to correct last night's mistake and make Nora trust him. He'd moved too fast with her. But she knew something and he was going to find out what. Too many of the trips E.J. had highlighted were escorted by Nora. Still, watching her sparkling eyes and soft mouth throughout dinner, he wished she weren't guilty.

What if she wasn't guilty? he continued to debate as they left the restaurant. He wasn't averse to getting her into bed, but then what? A man had only to look at Nora and know she wasn't interested in a quick affair—specifically, what was left of the bus tour. She was from a large family and probably wanted one of her own. She would pull out schedules from that ridiculous handbag of hers, boss everyone including her husband around, and they'd all love it. That had never been what Jake Collins wanted. He was a loner used to being in control.

"I try not to plan out everyone's life for them, honestly I don't, but I just can't help it." She turned her pleading, warm eyes on him and Jake hardened himself against her. "I always mean the best..." Nora trailed off and bit her bottom lip. She looked around in surprise. Once again, they were in front of her hotel-room door. She looked up expectantly, as if she wanted him to kiss her.

"We spend a lot time in this hallway," she said nervously. "I thought I saw you last night—" Jake pulled her to him, effectively cutting her off.

"We agreed to have a professional relationship," she protested even as her traitorous hands were smoothing the material of his shirt over his strong shoulders. *This is ridiculous, all the man has to do is touch me and I never want him to let me go.*

She waited for his lips to close the chasm between them. When he didn't, she dragged her gaze away from his tantalizing lips to his seductive eyes.

"We do have a professional relationship. This is just one of the perks."

His lips were gently sweet, discovering the taste and feel of her. Nora sighed with pleasure. She wanted him to hurry but was too caught up in the wonder to be able to take charge.

Jake ended the kiss much too soon. "Hell, you surprise me every time. No—" his finger lightly touched her lips "—don't say anything. I managed to spoil everything last night, let me leave before I do it again."

And he was gone. *Men!*

HOURS LATER, at the sound of a door opening, Jake hunched himself into an even smaller space in the alcove. The stately old Toronto hotel had a number of window seats that suited lovers or investigators. He had an admirable view of the corridor and the rooms of the Merry Travelers.

His right leg cramped, and he carefully eased it forward, rubbing the sore muscle. The glamorous life of the undercover agent usually meant too much time spent curled up in a small space. Long ago he'd learned how to sleep anywhere and wake at the slightest noise.

He wasn't tired so he calculated distances and gas mileage along their route. He was pretty sure Nora had chosen the wrong lunch stop on their way to Quebec City. In fact, he'd been looking over the routes for the other tours as well and had decided that Bruce Davis knew little about bus travel. Why, he could cut an hour's traveling time off every day. Maybe, after the case was over, Jake would send a letter to whoever was left running the company. If there was a company left....

Tonight the Merry Travelers seemed to have exhausted themselves. Jake was awakened only once— when Zachary Buch crept into Nora's room.

6

Today, enjoy a day of leisure in a city full of sight and activities. See some of the world's most famous buildings in this exciting cosmopolitan center.

"EVERYTHING IS FINE. Don't worry, Bruce, I have the situation under control." Nora was having difficulty keeping the exasperation out of her voice. Bruce Davis must have arrived at the Merry Travelers office at the crack of dawn to be phoning her this early. That wasn't like him. In fact, he'd never called her before. The office liked not to hear from a tour guide who was out on the road because it meant there weren't any problems with the trip. Bruce, certainly, hated to get himself involved. What had she said about this trip being strange . . . and getting stranger by the minute?

"Nothing unusual has happened?" Bruce demanded.

"Nothing—" Nora tried to placate her nervous boss "—except you could have warned me about the change of drivers."

"What do you mean? Isn't Bill Wilson your driver?"

"No. He's ill."

"Who's the replacement?"

"Jake Collins."

"Collins? We've never used a Collins before."

"That's because he's a rookie."

"A rookie!" Nora held the receiver away from her ear until Bruce's bellows diminished.

"Don't worry. Jake's good. We haven't had any problems."

"I don't like this, Nora. It's not like the charter company to replace a driver without informing us."

Silently Nora agreed. If Bruce had sent Jake to spy on her, he was putting on an Oscar-winning performance. "Calm down, Bruce, I have everything under control," she repeated.

"I hope so, Nora, I really hope so." Bruce quickly ended the conversation after extracting her promise to update him tomorrow. She looked around her hotel room. One double bed with a flowered comforter. A wicker chair by a round sitting table. The TV converter chained to the bedside table. She spent a lot of time in these interchangeable rooms in different cities, but soon she wouldn't have to. Soon she'd be her own boss.

Shaking off her worries, she left for the lobby where she was to meet the Reids, Molly and Holly. They were waiting for her, along with the Chance brothers.

"Here you are, dear." Molly pulled Nora aside and whispered confidentially, "Tim and John insisted on joining our outing today."

Recalling her ridiculous behavior of two nights ago, she signaled her thanks to Holly.

Molly continued: "I think one of them admires Holly."

"They're like Siamese twins joined on the same psychic wavelength. How can you tell who likes whom?"

"Trust me, when you've...been around as many men as I have, you develop senses six through ten about them. It's just how Mr. Collins— Why, there he is!" Molly smiled slyly at Nora. "I invited him to join us on our little excursion but I never thought— Try working on your sixth sense, dear. The others will follow." Molly turned to Jake. "I'm so glad you decided to join us. We're all paired up and now Nora will have company." With a surprisingly strong shove she pushed Nora toward Jake.

"I thought you'd have more exciting plans for your day off than playing tourist." She felt that familiar tingle as he turned his attention to her and she remembered Bruce's genuine surprise about the new driver. Her guilt had made her overly suspicious. Today, she was going to put all of that out of her mind and enjoy herself!

"What could be more exciting than spending the day with a beautiful woman in a world-class city?" Jake's reference to Toronto's obsession with being considered as good as its more famous competitors, like New York or Paris, made her chuckle and almost dispelled the rush of heat that had spread through her body at his description of her as beautiful.

Jake noted the becoming flush, satisfied his approach was working. Nora was wearing green walking shorts and a peachy pink blouse. It was sensible attire for a day of sight-seeing, Jake realized, but the shorts revealed a great butt and long legs. He'd love to test all of her curves and see if her face flushed as pink as her blouse. Under that competent, efficient manner was a passionate woman, and he was spending more and more time thinking about setting that woman free. He could imagine her biting her succulent bottom lip in passion to stop from moaning as he entered her. He'd pull her wounded lip into his mouth and treasure it and then take her over the edge until the people in the next room pounded on the walls. . . .

After last night's revelation he was determined to uncover her secrets. That too-innocent-and-sincere routine, including the book for black marks, wasn't going to fool him any longer. He had a job to do and he was going to get it done. If that included seducing her, well, that was just one of the perks of the job.

He took her elbow and steered her out of the hotel to the subway. Nora insisted the only real way to discover a city was to use its public transportation. And to talk to the people.

Nora was very good at talking to strangers, Jake discovered. She learned the hot dog vendor's eldest son was studying to become a doctor; the gardener at the hotel had fled to Canada from Poland in the early eighties and was now considering a visit home; and the ticket seller at Casa Loma was having trouble with her wedding plans.

And while Nora gave him a private tour of Casa Loma, Toronto's famed castle, and could relate its history with ease—in 1911 Sir Henry Pellatt spent over three million dollars to build a medieval-style castle and filled it with luxuries—she wasn't impressed by it. "Sir Henry had gold faucets put in his room and in the stables but only silver faucets in his wife's rooms. I've always thought that was very mean."

"Do you want gold faucets?"

"That's not what I meant. I think it's terrible that he would rank his wife as one of his possessions and consider her less valuable than his horses."

"Maybe his horses were more dependable."

At his bitter words, Nora said, "You must have been hurt very badly by a woman, Jake."

"We've all been hurt in the game between the sexes." He flashed his wicked smile. "But I've never been mortally wounded." He didn't get hurt because he never cared too much. Love was an overrated emotion when lovemaking was available.

"You see love as a game?"

"Nora, you're getting caught up on the words and missing my meaning." Jake looked around and saw that once again they were alone in a corridor. He decided to test himself and ran a finger along the soft skin of her cheek, pleased when she caught her breath. Good. He tried to ignore his own response as he let his fingers drift to her mouth and traced its outline.

"The attraction between a man and a woman is what's important. Discovering a beautiful woman, learning what she cares about—" now his fingers found their way to the hollow of her throat, testing the furiously beating pulse "—exploring her passion—that's what's important." Jake dipped his head and pressed his lips to her throat.

She smelled of green apples—her soap, he'd learned earlier when he'd searched her room while she was at breakfast. Nora trembled in his arms and he wondered just how passionate she would be in bed. Under all that control she was probably a wildcat. God, he couldn't wait—

"Help!"

With a curse, Jake turned and saw Holly running down the hallway.

"Jake, Nora, come quick!" Holly gasped. "Mrs. Reid has been robbed!" Jake stared into Nora's eyes and saw the same passion that had to be reflected in his, and he damned easy cases. "We'd better see what happened." He and Nora took off after the running Holly. They hurried to a courtyard surrounded by a stone fence where a sobbing Mrs. Reid, her wig askew yet again, was being comforted by her husband.

"What happened?" Jake quietly asked the frightened woman.

"I was mugged. He took my ring—my beautiful anniversary ring!"

"How did it happen?" Jake's even tone calmed Mrs. Reid, and she recounted how a young man with long dark hair and one dangling silver earring had accosted her.

"He took my ring," she finished pitifully. "We never had the money for an engagement ring but Hank saved and saved and gave me the ring when he retired. He said it was my reward for putting up with him for forty-five years. And now it's gone."

Nora knelt down next to Mrs. Reid and patted the sobbing woman's hand. "It'll be all right, Mrs. Reid. The police will be here soon and I'm sure they'll be able to get your ring back." She looked at Jake for reassurance.

He shook his head.

Nora knew he was right and that her optimistic words had little hope of coming true. Despondently she gazed at the small crowd gathered around them. As she studied their curious and interested faces she glimpsed a man moving away from the crowd, the sun glinting off his long dangling earring. Her surprised gasp caught Mrs. Reid's attention and the woman's grasp on Nora's hand tightened. "That's him," she breathed. "That's the man who mugged me."

"Jake," Nora began, but he was already fighting his way through the crowd.

Mrs. Reid's assailant broke into a run with Jake at his heels, and Nora only slightly farther back. She lost them for a moment as they disappeared behind the corner of a building and she heard the sound of a muffled shout.

As she rounded the building, she saw Jake and the suspect on the ground grappling together. Like the heroine in a bad melodrama she silently watched the two men fighting, helpless to do anything. Where were the damned police? she wondered, as she looked for a large rock and an opening to hit the mugger.

By the time she'd found her rock, Jake had the suspect pinned beneath him and his hands around the man's throat.

"Who sent you?" Jake asked in an ice-cold voice that frightened Nora.

Desperation must have given the man extra strength because he managed to free an arm, punch Jake in the stomach and roll away. Nora threw her rock and managed to graze the side of his head.

"What the—?" he exclaimed in surprise and looked for his unexpected assailant. She backed up, fearful of the dangerous glint in the young man's eyes.

"Don't even think about it." Jake was back on his feet moving toward the thug. The man turned to Jake, and Nora finally heard the wail of a police siren. So did the mugger as he hesitated and then reached inside his jacket.

"No!" Nora screamed and launched herself at him and, in surprise, he turned toward her again. His hand shot out, and she felt the world tilt away, then hit her— hard.

Dimly, Nora heard Jake calling to her as if through a muffled speaker. Then she became aware that Jake was cradling her head on his knees. When his face came back into focus, she smiled at him, relieved she had saved him.

"That was a really stupid thing to do," Jake said. She pushed herself away from him.

"I thought he was going for a gun."

"So you drew his attention to yourself! Of all the harebrained, foolish acts I've seen—" Jake glared at her. "If you ever do anything like that again, I'll throttle you myself!"

Nora couldn't believe him. She'd practically rescued him from the clutches of death and he was yelling at her! "Don't you threaten me, Jake Collins—" She was suddenly aware of the crowd of excited people surrounding them.

The commotion had attracted what seemed to be every tourist at Casa Loma. Several were taking photographs of herself and Jake. Holly broke through the mob and put a supporting arm around Nora, and Nora gladly leaned into her comfort.

Nora was only aware of the ensuing events in small scenes. Holly found the aspirin and bottled water in Nora's purse for her and that eased her throbbing head a little. Then the police were there taking statements. She declined a trip to the hospital, wanting only to get back to her room where she could be alone to analyze the feeling of dread that had overtaken her when she'd thought Jake was about to be killed. Then a once-again-sobbing Mrs. Reid had thrown her arms around Jake's neck, thanking him again and again for the return of her ring.

"Mrs. Reid's ring?" Nora asked Holly.

"Yes, dear. Oh, you must have missed it in all the action but when the robber realized Jake was about to take him he threw it away so he could make his getaway."

"He threw the ring away?"

"Yes, he took it out of his jacket pocket and threw it. But how did you get hit, love?"

"Just bad luck, I guess," Nora muttered.

When the police had finished, she and Holly took a taxi back to the hotel. Nora declined the older woman's kind offer to stay with her and retreated to the privacy of her room.

One look in the mirror at her grass-stained and ripped blouse and dirt-streaked face had her tearing off her clothes and running a tub. Flexing her jaw was painful so she carefully repeated the action several times.

Soaking in the hot water Nora closed her eyes and let the sequence of events replay themselves again and again. She felt her fear anew when she relived the moment she'd believed Jake was about to be shot or knifed or . . . something. It would have served him right.

What she had felt was no more than if it had been a complete stranger. And if it had been a stranger she would have been even more concerned—she didn't even like Jake Collins. He was cold, unfeeling and he never smiled!

He had also known exactly what to do.

Nora opened her eyes at that thought. Jake's questioning of Mrs. Reid had been soothing and . . . professional. He'd fought against his attacker like he was trained to do so.

Like a trained professional.

No, she thought in horror. Bruce wouldn't do this to her. He wouldn't send a professional investigator to spy on her. Would he?

Yes, she was forced to admit, Bruce was capable of exactly that if he believed his business was threatened.

And wasn't that exactly what she was guilty of?

7

Your trip begins as soon as you board our coach. Along with the wonderful stops is the sheer entertainment of traveling. And don't forget board games and seat rotation so you can meet fellow travelers. That's why over half of our passengers are repeat clientele!

AFTER A RESTLESS SLEEP that was filled with dreams about her being locked up behind bars while Jake Collins threw away the key, Nora was alone on the bus early Wednesday morning, searching through her bag for that day's assortment of bus games and crossword books. Next to her mace and her curling iron she found Peter's phone number. When had he slipped that into her bag? Still puzzling over the slip of paper, her neck began to tingle. She waited for the guilty heat to die down on her face before saying in a remarkably strong voice, "You're good at sneaking up on people. I never hear you behind me."

"But you know I'm here."

"Yes." She turned and studied Jake, using her new knowledge of him as a measuring stick. He had a strong face that spoke of having seen and done a lot. The muscled body revealed a man who kept himself fit and ready. But most striking was the keen intelligence, the way he observed and assessed. Yes, Bruce Davis could definitely have hired Jake Collins to spy on her. That was a problem that she didn't know how to solve. She couldn't just ask, "Excuse me, but did Bruce hire you because he suspects . . . ?"

She hadn't wanted to believe Zachary's suspicions but yesterday had proved her wrong. And she was so close to finishing the deal! Three last trips and she would have been set.

She still felt like she was double-crossing Bruce Davis, but as Zachary had so eloquently argued, between drinks, she could run a company better than Bruce. And she was going to, she decided. Jake Collins was not going to stop her.

Competition was the American way, Zachary had slurringly declared. The rival charter company he and Nora were opening would give Bruce a lot to worry about, but Nora had never realized before yesterday that the bus business actually had spies! An incognito James Bond behind the wheel!

The other problem was the electricity Jake sent out. The very air around him was charged with energy, seeping into her body, giving her pulse a workout. From the way his eyes narrowed as he considered her answer, she suspected he felt a similar kind of response. Could she use this to her advantage?

Her other dreams last night had all been erotic—certainly no prison bars had separated her from Jake. She and Jake had been together on the bus, driving through the countryside. On a secluded stretch of road he'd stopped, left the driver's seat and come toward her, throwing off his driver's cap, undoing his tie, unbuttoning his shirt to reveal a hard, muscular chest. She'd just sat there watching him come for her.

He'd taken the bow out of her hair—she'd been wearing the Merry Travelers nightmare-in-pink uniform—and run the suede across her lips and then down along her neck, into the vee between her breasts. And then his mouth and hands had been everywhere, kissing her, tearing off her clothes, pleasing her—

Get a grip, Nora told herself. Obviously Jake Collins was on Bus Tour 626 for reasons of his own. No matter how much she'd tried to discount her theory that Bruce Davis had sent Jake to spy on her, she couldn't ultimately deny the truth. In the early-morning hours, however, she'd decided she had to stay as far away from Jake as possible.

He was flirting with her to disorient her—very successfully, she admitted—to get her guard down.

But with Jake standing so close to her, all she could think of was how she wanted to drag him down to the floor and show him just how exciting a bus ride could be.

No, that was the Nora who had her heart broken by good-time guys.

And Jake Collins was a good time if she'd ever seen one.

"We have a problem," Jake said.

Expecting another argument over the day's route, Nora turned to him with what she hoped was a serene expression on her face. She was confident she could keep a tight rein on her desires, until she saw the look on Jake's face.

He was looking at her as though he couldn't decide which piece of clothing to take off first, and whether they should do it standing up or on the floor. Nora gulped and turned to flee.

He caught her arm and pulled her toward him. They stood together, chest to chest, hip to hip, absorbing the possibilities of one another. He smelled like pine—from the bathroom cleaner, she knew—but its effect was erotic. She closed her eyes to inhale another lungful.

How had Jake gotten to her so quickly? It had to be some weird chemical reaction—he did smell good!— that had her behaving so oddly. She knew Jake was giving her every chance to leave, but she just couldn't.

She could lie to herself about why it would be reasonable, smart even, to sleep with Jake. One, it would give her control. Two, it might get him out of her system. Three, maybe she'd find out what he was up to— no pun intended. But all that really mattered was that she wanted to very, very much.

Jake backed up. She followed and lost track of whatever else it was she wanted to say as she rose on tiptoe, put her hand on his shoulder and nibbled his ear. "You smell really good." She discovered that if she moved her head just so, she could scrape her teeth along his jaw and—

That was all the encouragement Jake needed. Nora didn't know what happened, except their positions reversed and she found herself wedged between the wall and Jake's strong body. He kissed her long and hard, and she forgot everything except how good it felt to be in his arms, how right it felt to have him touching her.

Nora moaned as his lips skimmed her neck and then his tongue flicked in and out of her earlobe. One hand was tracing the line separating silk and flesh on her buttocks. He groaned and pulled her leg up around his waist so he could push himself against her. She was all too aware of his arousal and her own. He repeated his actions a second and third time and Nora heard a whimpering sound leave her throat. She pulled his mouth back to her so she could kiss him, her last thoughts of control leaving her. She challenged him, dared him to want as much as she did. She ran her hands over his back, his shoulders, trying to memorize the feel of him. Her body was all sensation, aches and needs desperate to be fulfilled.

Their clothing made their awkward, teasing joining torture. Jake was skimming his fingers along her inner thigh, and she knew she would die if he didn't touch her.

Jake pulled away from their soul-draining kiss and stared at her as he teased her sensitive flesh. Nora felt the proof of her own desire—she who had never experienced passion this quickly before. She quivered as he first lightly stroked over her, then into her.

All the time their eyes remained locked. He was giving her every chance to stop, to admit she was only playing a dangerous game. Instead Nora grabbed his belt buckle and undid it. She began to unzip his pants, slowly, notch by notch, watching the surprise fade from his eyes, to be replaced by heat, all-consuming fire that threatened to consume her. She smiled—

Jake cursed and pushed her away.

"What?" Nora demanded in a daze, only to become aware of the furious knocking on the bus door.

"We have an audience." Jake indicated the crowd outside, led by an angry Alicia Hall.

Nora was having a hard time recovering her senses. Jake seemed to be having a similar problem. "You'd better let them on board," she ground out between clenched teeth. Of all the times for her roving seniors to become clock conscious!

Jake nodded and headed to the door. He stopped with his hand on the lever and turned those dangerous eyes on her. "Tonight, let's have dinner—" as the rapping increased in volume he grimaced "—alone."

"I— Yes."

The pounding threatened to knock the door down. Jake cursed and opened it.

Alicia Hall swept onto the bus like an arctic blast over Canada. "If we don't leave now, we'll be late. Whatever were you thinking of, Nora? There's lots of time for fooling around later." Alicia commandeered a seat up front—probably to keep an eye on her and Jake— and ordered the other seniors on board. Before Nora could do more than look embarrassed, before she could even begin to analyze what had happened between her and Jake, Alicia had the bus heading toward Montreal.

SEXUAL COMBUSTION.

That's what it was, Jake decided.

They made movies about overpowering lust all the time. *Body Heat, Fatal Attraction.* Unfortunately, those stories didn't have much of a happy ending: a man so obsessed by a woman, he lost all self-control.

He hadn't totally lost control, although if Alicia hadn't stormed the bus . . . He remembered every taste, every quiver Nora had made.

He checked the mirror for traffic, then angled it so he could see the group. Nora sat by herself, her face pink, apparently lost in thought. Remembering?

He'd never had a response to a woman like that before. Nora Stevens might not look like a man-killer, but that long, daring look just before— He'd wanted to make her beg.

What the hell was he going to do?

This simple case was turning out to be not so simple, after all. The bus search had revealed nothing and he was still going through the Merry Travelers' hotel rooms. He'd found nothing incriminating so far.

He eyed Nora's multicolored tote. It never left her side. Continuing to scan the bus he found Molly staring at him. She flashed him a victory sign. If that amorous sexagenarian found him searching her room, he'd be lucky to escape with his virtue intact.

He hunkered down in his seat. He definitely didn't like everyone directing—much less being aware of—his love life. No one at headquarters knew when he was involved with a woman—which was just how he liked it. He was a loner, he reminded himself, he liked to do his own pursuing. And women who wanted a future bored him. Before D.C., he'd skated close to permanency with Mary, had even thought about marrying her, but when he realized that she expected to live in one city, for him to get a permanent desk job, he'd ended it. He loved the possibilities still ahead for him. A mortgage and diapers meant a slow death.

Even worse was being involved with a bossy woman like— "What?" he asked, realizing Nora had spoken.

"I said," she began very slowly, "where are we?"

Jake suddenly noticed how quiet the bus was. The animated game of bingo that had been going on forever had stopped. Twelve pairs of eyes stared at him. In front, the road was no longer a modern expressway but a one-lane track that was threatening to turn into a goat path.

"Oh."

"How long have we been on this road?" Nora inquired.

"I have no idea," Jake admitted. "I was thinking about—something else."

Nora blushed.

A strident voice demanded, "Are we lost? Really, Nora, we don't have time for this, we're on a tight enough schedule as it is."

"Don't worry, Mrs. Hall." Nora hurried over to Alicia. "Jake likes to take the scenic route." After a few minutes of assuring the group that they were indeed on the right road, she stood on the steps next to Jake. "Figured out where we are yet?"

"No," he answered glumly. What was wrong with him? He'd never been lost in his life. "I'm really sorry. I wasn't paying any attention." He began to slow the bus.

Nora grabbed the rail in front of her. "What are you doing?"

"Turning the bus around."

"We'll get stuck in a ditch if you try it here. Keep going till we find a farm. And keep looking for signs!"

They continued for several more miles. Nora took the microphone and began to give an inspired lecture on the trees and geography of Ontario. When Jake finally found a farm road to turn around on, he smiled. Turning to Nora, he asked for the mike. With a quirked eyebrow, she passed it over. He parked under a shady tree.

"Ladies and gentlemen, I haven't been blueberry picking since I was a little kid on my parents' farm. This is too good an opportunity to miss." At the puzzled exclamations from the seniors, he waved toward the field, "Blueberries, as far as you can see. We'll take a forty-five-minute break so that we can all gather some berries."

An excited hubbub broke out as the Merry Travelers began to share memories of berry picking as children. Nora reached into her purse and found a box of industrial-strength plastic bags and distributed them to everyone exiting the bus.

"That was inspired," she said to Jake when they were the only two left onboard.

He smiled. "I've been told I was a good kisser, but never inspired."

"The blueberries, you egotistical fool."

"Oh, those." He waved his hand dismissively.

"Did you really have a farm?" Nora realized that this was the first piece of information Jake had volunteered about himself.

"For a long time." He smiled that lethal smile.

She needed to get away from him and assess what had almost happened between them. She'd think it all through logically, decide upon an appropriate course of action. "While I pick some berries—" Nora slapped on a sunhat "—you can go over the map and figure out where we are."

"Yes, boss." He saluted.

Nora knew her new strategy would work perfectly—until Jake kissed her again.

AN HOUR LATER the berry pickers were back on the bus, merrily chattering away. Eleven bags of berries rested on the last seat. Alicia Hall had refused to participate; she had stood by the bus, glaring at her watch. When Nora began passing out the bingo cards, Alicia refused her scorecard. "Really, this is too much fun and games, Nora. We'll be hours late arriving into Montreal. I'm going to write and complain to your superiors."

"Oh, hush, you old biddy!" Zachary hiccuped. "Have a swig, it'll loosen you up." He offered a wine-skin, but Nora intercepted.

"I don't think Mrs. Hall is interested," she quietly in-sisted, steering Zachary back to his seat.

"Well, then, this lovely lady is," he said, plopping down beside Holly. Molly was sitting with Stephan Papas.

Nora recalled that Zachary and Holly's blueberry pickings were mighty slim when they'd returned gig-gling from the woods. She eyed the berry stains on Holly's dress. She was traveling with a group of love-sick fools.

Why, those two were no better than her and Jake.

HOURS LATER, the Merry Travelers reached the hotel in Montreal and scattered. Nora ran to her room, threw down her bag and hurried back to the lobby to follow Jake. She wanted to know how Jake Collins filled the time before their date. Despite the lecture she'd given herself about using the attraction between Jake and herself, Nora's pulse raced at the thought of an evening alone with him. She wanted to know whether he was spying on her or not. Whether this would affect her de-sire to sleep with him, she had no idea.

Sunk low in one of the extremely modern-looking lobby chairs, newspaper held high, she watched her passengers form into groups and leave. Molly and Holly went off with Stephan Papas. Tim and John

Chance disappeared into the hotel bar. Ben Riley returned from outside and stood in the lobby, waiting.

"Looking for anyone in particular?" Jake asked from the chair next to her. He flashed a wicked grin at someone behind her. Nora turned to see a far-too-chic reservations clerk winking at Jake. Did women everywhere have to swoon all over him? And did he have to be so blatant with his charms?

"Or were you looking for me?"

"You." Nora decided she'd make a terrible spy. She couldn't even find Jake right out in the open.

"Come on—" Jake stood and held out a hand "—let's take a walk."

The cobblestone streets of Old Montreal had always held a special charm for Nora as if she could touch the past. She'd imagined walking here with a lover, sharing dreams and secrets. Unfortunately, she'd been so busy, and determined to become successful, that she'd never found a man to invite. Jake fit the image very nicely—except that she couldn't trust him. And she certainly couldn't trust herself.

He held her hand, and they peered in shop windows and looked at the people in the cafés looking at everyone else.

"Where did you live before Washington?" Nora asked.

"All around. I've never found a place that feels right for long. I always want to move to see what's next. I was a cook in Alaska, dealt cards in Vegas, worked on a cruise ship, whatever was available." All arranged as covers, courtesy of the U.S. government.

A man without roots, Nora realized. Jake Collins would be interested in a fling, nothing more. As her neck tingled when he smiled at her, she knew she was behaving foolishly. One minute she believed Jake was the Clint Eastwood of the bus trade, the next that she was a paranoid fool.

"What about family?" she asked.

"Only child. My father was a farmer, but he died when I was in high school, and we lost the farm."

"Don't you get tired of it? Want to have a place that's your home?"

"No." Jake considered for a moment. "The farm cost my parents too much. All they did was work, and they never got any further ahead. It sucked them dry and killed my father. My mother didn't have anything after he died."

"She had you."

"I could never replace my father. But I could get work that would help her out financially. Still, I don't want to get tied down like they did. It's why I like the road." He dreamed of what could happen next, what might be around the next corner. Nora wanted security and Jake had a sudden need to make sure she understood the differences between them. "You must dream of a home and a family."

Nora turned to look in a store window. "Sometimes," she admitted.

The rest of the day went far too quickly for Nora. They saw a few of their passengers: Zachary Buch taking notes on the port, Alicia and Ben leaving a bank, Holly and Molly eating in a café with Stephan Papas. Parts of it, like how Jake smiled at her over dinner, were imprinted on her memory forever. But other parts went by in an amazing blur, so that she was vaguely surprised to discover it was midnight when they were once again in the corridor—this one decorated in muted shades of gray and black to match the modern decor of the hotel—in front of her room.

"A hotel corridor," she teased. "I thought I saw you out here the first night, keeping track of our merry revelers playing bedroom tag."

"We could play our own version of bedroom tag." He brushed her hair back over her shoulder and stroked her neck.

Nora caught her breath at the desire in his eyes. Her neck tingled. He wanted her but he wasn't going to push.

And she finally admitted how much she wanted him. She was going to throw her usual caution out the window. "Yes," she said simply and unlocked her door.

"Nora, love, you're finally here," said Bruce Davis, stretched out on top of her bed.

8

Every day is full of surprises on the road! Turn around that corner, and you'll discover the most breathtaking view, quaint café or shop with the best bargains. Come prepared to enjoy the unexpected!

"WHAT ARE YOU doing here?"

"I've come to see you, love."

"I mean, what are you doing in my room?" Nora wasn't sure if she was angrier at Bruce or at Jake, who was radiating disapproval.

"The hotel is all booked up. I was waiting here while they tried to find me a room," Bruce answered smoothly as he stood, adjusting a crease in his linen trousers. He peered down at his shoes, probably trying to catch his balding reflection in their four-hundred-dollar shine, Jake thought. He studied the two and couldn't imagine them together but that was probably wishful thinking. Bruce was fit, well-dressed and had an all-American smile. E.J. had called him a smooth operator. Jake disliked him immediately.

Nora looked as if she was as frustrated as he felt. But she could be disappointed that she hadn't seduced him and gained his confidence. Jake wished he didn't question everyone's motives, but that was what made him a good investigator.

Bruce pecked Nora on the cheek in greeting. What was between those two? Jake knew the young thug who had stolen Mrs. Reid's ring had to have been one of Lucci's men, sent to distract him from the main investigation. Unfortunately, it was logical that Nora was the person who had tipped off Lucci about him. No one else had reason to be suspicious.

"Bruce, I'm more than a little surprised to see you here. *Why* did you come?"

"Ah, Nora, I just wanted to make sure everything was okay. A surprise check, if you will."

"A surprise check! You've never done anything like this before."

"No time like the present to start."

Color high, Nora stormed to the door and opened it. "You can start right now by finding your own room. I want the two of you out *now*." At the quirk of Jake's eyebrow, she turned on him. "Don't think I don't know what your suspicious mind was thinking."

"But Nora, I don't have any place to sleep," Bruce sputtered.

Nora picked up his Gucci bag and threw it at him. "And take him—" she pointed at Jake "—with you. If you ask nicely, maybe you can share his room. The two of you deserve each other!"

IF HE DESERVED Bruce Davis for a roommate, Jake contemplated morosely from the cold window recess, he must have done something especially nasty in a past life.

The Merry Travelers were up to their nightly ritual—a scurried exchange of rooms. Molly had once again disappeared with Stephan, and Holly had arrived with a mystery man. He'd thought she had a thing going with Zachary. Remembering Zachary's visit to Nora's room, Jake grimaced. Surely Nora and Zachary couldn't be having an affair! But what was the alternative? Everybody couldn't be part of the crime ring.

In the muffled, well-carpeted hall he heard a door open. Alicia Hall made her way down the corridor and stopped in front of room 112—that of Ben Riley and Harold Anderson. Ben appeared, unbidden, a few minutes later. Ben and Alicia held a brief but agitated dialogue that Jake was unable to overhear. Whatever the issue was didn't seem to be resolved but the argument ended with a passionate kiss and a grope. They then returned to their separate rooms.

Several more fruitless hours had Jake returning to his room, but his newly acquired roommate had already left. A quick search of Bruce's belongings revealed nothing except that the owner of Merry Travelers had a fondness for flowered boxer shorts—a gift from a woman? Nora? Then Jake was off in search of the two.

"IT LOOKS LIKE SOMEBODY slipped some raw herring into their eggs," said Molly, pointing at the unfriendly threesome of Bruce, Nora and Jake breakfasting in a nearby booth.

"Or vinegar in their tea," replied the more British-minded Holly. "Why do you suppose Bruce Davis is here? And why is he putting his arm around Nora? He's ruining all of our plans!"

"You've never heard any rumors of a liaison between Nora and Bruce?"

"Never!"

"Neither have I, and if we haven't heard anything then there's nothing between them," Molly decided firmly. "But there's something very odd going on here. Why, last night, I was going to get some ice to chill the wine, but when I opened the door I saw Alicia and Ben kissing! Well, you can imagine my shock! I practically dropped the ice bucket, which would have been awful because then I wouldn't have heard what they said."

Holly very slowly sipped her tea, wiped the corners of her mouth and pulled out her lipstick and reapplied it. Then she turned to her friend. "You always have to dramatize everything. It would serve you right if I don't ask what you heard—you'd die from trying to keep it inside. Then the death certificate could list cause of death as too much curiosity."

"Holly!"

"All right, what did you hear?"

"Alicia told Ben not to worry, that Jake would be taken care of."

In unison they turned their attention back to Jake's table. Nora was glaring at Bruce, who seemed to be arguing with her. Jake was sitting back, taking it all in.

"But that's talk straight out of a gangster movie!" Holly exclaimed. "Although, I must admit that if I were casting the role of an FBI agent, Jake would be my first choice. Why, those broad shoulders, those muscular thighs, that hard look that sometimes seems so sad, the way he can look at Bruce and Nora and still study the whole room, the way he's always in the corridor late at night, the way he handled that mugger . . ." Holly cast disbelieving eyes on her table companion. "He couldn't be, could he?"

"This is too exciting!" Molly practically jumped up and down in her seat. "Oh, it's just too perfect. Imagine, we worried doing a trip the second time around would be dull. We have our very own secret agent!"

"No, Molly, we don't know for sure. It's just speculation." Holly savored the words.

"What else explains what's going on? Maybe one of us is a defecting—"

"A defecting what? There's no place left to defect from."

"Diamonds!"

"What are you talking about?"

"I saw it on a movie-of-the-week. Diamond smuggling! Montreal is notorious as a center for diamond brokers."

"I saw that! You're on to something." Holly poured more tea into her cup and stirred it furiously, clinking against the porcelain for almost a minute, until she had absorbed all the information. "Maybe Mrs. Reid's attacker wasn't just a mugger," she said, testing the words slowly. "He was, after all, stealing her *diamond* ring."

"You're right! Oh, we're definitely on to something big. But the Reids? They seem so nice—why would they have worked so hard in that grocery store if they're world-famous smugglers?"

"As a cover. And, let me remind you, have we ever *seen* their grocery store?"

"Holly, last night at dinner, Mrs. Reid didn't know the different kinds of lettuce in our salad. She claimed she always got confused, but after forty years at the checkout you'd know your arugula from your radicchio!"

The two swung their heads in unison toward the table where the Reids were eating with Zachary Buch. "Zachary Buch, that's a phony name if ever I heard one. Buch means book in German!" Holly snorted. She continued staring at him until Zachary raised his head, saw her and flushed. "See, he even looks guilty!"

"And Taylor means a tailor but that doesn't make Elizabeth a seamstress or guilty of any crime except choosing bad husbands and putting on too much eyeliner," Molly pointed out practically. "Holly, he thinks you like him. He is kind of cute...but what about what I overheard last night?"

Holly nodded in agreement. "There are a lot of suspects. Have you ever noticed how much jewelry Janet Rule wears? She claims they're cubic zirconias from the shopping network, but what if they're not? The best way to smuggle something is out in the open."

"And the Chance brothers. I thought they were following us but that could be a smoke screen. Neither has made a move." Molly considered her friend. "Has one?"

"No. And we can't forget Stephan."

"Stephan!" Molly resorted to one of her grandchildren's favorite expressions. "Get with the program, Holly. Stephan is a wonderful man, loving and caring. Why, he's visiting his relatives today and taking them out to dinner."

"Then you'd better get yourself invited along, because on the last trip he told me he didn't know anyone in Montreal."

"Oh, my, that rotten, lying—!"

"Molly, calm down, maybe it's nothing," Holly attempted to placate her infuriated friend. After Molly had gone over the various merits of different tortures for Stephan, Holly outlined her plan. "You'd better go off with Stephan while I stick to the Reids like denture cream."

"WHY ARE THOSE TWO OLD biddies staring at me?" Bruce asked Nora as they walked out the door of the coffee shop.

"They probably want to thank you for their free trip," she retorted acerbically. Bruce looked away and tried to scrunch himself behind a large potted plant. Molly and Holly hurried purposefully past the other side. When the two were gone, Bruce straightened, then smiled at Nora ruefully.

"Er, yes," he said. "They're good customers and I thought we needed a new promotion."

"Giving away trips? Bruce, I've been wanting to talk to you about . . ." What could she ask him? Her questions might lead to his asking some uncomfortable ones about her. Nora studied him, wondering if he'd really hired Jake to investigate her. Bruce's brown eyes usually brimmed with his ready laugh. He was tall and slim, capturing a lot of female attention. He looked equally good in a well-tailored business suit or in his more casual attire of jeans and oxford shirt, like today. At times, Nora and the other female employees of Merry Travelers had giggled over Bruce Davis—he was the last Yuppie holdout. He played all the right sports: squash, racquetball and golf, was equally well-read when it came to both the latest "I-did-it-all-myself-and-you-can-too ghostwritten autobiography and the menu of the current chichi restaurant, and he liked to buy high-tech gadgets for his kitchen. For Bruce, the eighties hadn't ended.

Maybe it was time to be honest with Bruce and then she could sleep at night. But there wasn't any need to spill the beans first! "Bruce, I'd like to help you. Talk to me." Nora put a hand on his arm; his gaze held hers questioningly.

He opened his mouth, closed it, then began, "Nora I don't—"

"Bruce Davis, what an unexpected pleasure," interrupted Zachary, his round face beaming as he exuberantly pumped the startled man's hand. Bruce looked

puzzled by Zachary, clearly searching his memory to
see if they had ever met. Nora knew they hadn't; it was
just her friend checking up on her. She wished he wasn't
so interfering.

"Oh, yes, a pleasure, Mr.?—" Bruce tried. He looked
to Nora for help.

"Buch, Zachary Buch. I've been on several of your
wonderful trips. I recognized your photograph from the
brochure." Zachary threw a hearty arm around Bruce's
shoulder and started to steer him away. "You must have
a million fascinating stories...."

Nora watched Zachary drag off the hapless Bruce
Davis. "Damn!"

"Your plans gone awry?" Jake's voice questioned
softly.

"Everything is damn weird, Jake Collins, ever since
you showed up. And stop sneaking up on me!" Nora's
frustration exploded. Jake's face hardened until she
couldn't read anything, and just as quickly her anger
disappeared. She pushed a hand through her hair.
"Jake, I'm sorry, I didn't mean to attack you. My nerves
are shot."

To put it mildly. Her cohort in crime had just gone
off with the man they were more or less about to dou-
ble-cross—only Bruce was up to some tricks of his own.
Why was this tour running at all? Was Jake just an ordinary great-looking guy? Did she want to sleep with
him or didn't she?

She sighed. She wasn't used to having so many questions with so few answers. Well, Nora resolved, she'd

try to get some answers from Jake first and then . . . well . . . whatever. It was time to begin. "Some of the passengers wanted to tour Chez Marie—home of the maple syrup queen. It's an original log house about twenty miles outside of Montreal where they bake bread and serve it with maple butter and then you can buy the products. It's not on the agenda but we can go if I convince the driver to take us." She would have smiled pleadingly but that might have tipped him off.

"It's customary to visit Chez Marie?"

"Almost every trip." Nora held her breath.

"What time do you want the bus?"

"At eleven. You won't regret it," Nora promised as she told herself this was one bus ride Jake Collins wouldn't forget.

9

Every day is a new adventure. Prepare to put aside
your old ideas and experience something new!

JAKE PULLED THE BUS up to the hotel and nodded to another driver. So far his fraternization with them had
provided little new information. These men—few
women had broken into the ranks—enjoyed the freedom of the road and offered advice on how to increase
tips and kickbacks.

The drivers and escorts were preoccupied with finding ways to supplement their income. Not that he could
blame them. The world of bus nomads was divided
along sexual lines. The drivers were men, unionized
and respectably paid, even receiving a food allowance.
The escorts were usually women and were expected to
consider their enjoyment of travel part of their pay-
ment. Their salaries were very low, usually under sev-
enty-five dollars for a commonplace ten-hour day, with
no food allowance. Instead, most escorts were experts
at arranging group meals where they could eat for free.

The escorts, or tour coordinators as Nora preferred
they be called, were a similar kind. Little Miss Merry
Sunshines, using the force of their own personalities to
bond together a disparate band of people. Nora was a

perfect example, he considered, as he watched her make her way to the bus. Her shoulder-length hair was loose and curled attractively around her face. This morning her hair had been clipped back so she had obviously made time to style it. She was wearing a short gauzy skirt that swirled around her long legs as she stopped to chat with one of the bellboys. Nora knew most of the hotel workers.

But Nora's constantly cheerful facade wasn't all an act. She wasn't capable of assuming a completely different persona as he was. So how was she mixed up with Bruce Davis?

Bruce's surprise visit hadn't fooled Jake for a minute. Nora had been genuinely taken aback, but that was undoubtedly at Bruce's bad timing. Just when she'd had Jake where she'd wanted him. And where *he'd* wanted to be, damn it!

He'd spent far too long last night thinking about kissing Nora, touching her, finding out if she was wearing that pink scrap of lace underneath her clothes. Finishing her conversation, Nora hurried to the bus and handed Jake a large basket. "I'll be right back," she said and ran back into the hotel. Nora always liked to do things in a hurry, Jake noted, as he wondered what she was planning. She returned carrying a portable cooler, which she deposited on the front seat.

"We're all set." Her voice sounded nervous.

"Where are our happy rovers?"

"They're not coming. It's just you and me." Nora wouldn't meet his eyes.

"There's no trip to Chez Marie?"

"No, but—"

"But, what?" Jake was pleased that his tone remained even, despite the fact he was seething. He had expected to learn something from this supposedly regular outing. At the least, he could have kept track of some of his roving suspects. Without Nora's interference he'd be trailing *somebody*—he'd seen Zachary Buch and Bruce Davis heading off together.

Nora tried out a smile on him. "I wanted us to have a picnic."

"Why?"

Nora's face flushed a pink that would have rivaled her Merry Travelers uniform and she took a deep breath. "Last night we... I... I wanted for us to be alone."

Standing in the shadows, waiting for the exact moment to take down a drug smuggler didn't accelerate his pulse as quickly. Last night they would have gone to bed. In his experience, if the moment was lost, that was it. He rarely cared enough to pursue any woman with a great deal of effort. And it never mattered much. If one woman said no, another was likely to say yes. He preferred the ease of those relationships—there were no messy endings; no long-term commitments to family and home.

The fact that he'd been with U.S. Customs for such a long time wasn't contradictory. The job offered a lot of freedom, a lot of movement. He was never trapped. Growing up on the farm, depending upon the weather for a good harvest, watching the strain it wrought between his parents, Jake had vowed to find a different kind of living—where he'd be pitting his wits against man, not nature.

Nora was different from him. She wasn't the kind to enjoy a short affair and happily say goodbye a few days later. If she was innocent, involvement with her created all kinds of danger for him—she could blindside him with the force of her emotions if he wasn't very careful. He was always a very careful man. It was time to change tactics and scare her off.

He turned what he knew could be a very cold gaze on her and announced, "You want to have sex with me."

"Yes."

The words were almost a whisper but he heard them and waited for her qualification: *But I want to get to know you better.* When the words didn't materialize, he realized that he had already missed the danger signs and was on a loaded minefield.

What the hell was she thinking? This wasn't like her. He was convinced of that. Obviously, she was gambling on something. The question was what. He had a hell of a lot of questions and no answers.

But he'd never been one to back down from a challenge. He shifted the bus into Drive and said, "I'm all yours. Lead the way."

JAKE SETTLED the blanket under the shade of a large maple tree while Nora unpacked the picnic hamper. An assortment of food came out of it: cheeses, crackers, pâté and fried chicken.

"Fried chicken?" he asked.

"I told the hotel chef I was going on a picnic. He insisted chicken was traditional." Her voice was shaky and she only darted glances at him.

"Nora—" he interrupted her recitation of their menu "—look at me." He cupped her chin gently and forced her to face him. "Don't worry, I'm not going to jump you. Relax and enjoy the day." He was surprised that he meant it—he didn't like making Nora so nervous. Instead, he wanted to comfort her. Where was his cool professionalism when he needed it? "I don't remember the last time I was on a picnic." It was nice out here in the open field, the daisies bobbing up and down in the wind.

"What do you usually do for fun?"

"I like mountain climbing, parachuting, kayaking. But I don't get to go as often as I'd like."

Doing any one of those things just once, would be more than enough, Nora thought. But Jake would like the excitement, the thrill, the challenge. And she was sure that he always won.

"Then I'm surprised driving a bus full of senior citizens isn't too sedate for you."

"It won't be a permanent job but so far it's been one surprise after another. Besides, I have to earn the money to indulge in my exotic passions."

The husky note in his last word brought Nora's eyes to his. His smoky gray eyes burned her. Mesmerized, she forgot to breathe. How could this man affect her so much without even touching her? He looked away and with unspoken consent they began to eat. Jake opened the wine and poured. Out in the open, with the scent of wildflowers wafting on the breeze, he felt himself begin to relax for the first time in a long time. He could almost imagine what it would be like to be on a regular date with Nora.

"Tell me about your family." He meant the words as a distraction and then was surprised that he genuinely wanted to know.

"Five kids. I'm the eldest. I have two brothers and two sisters, who are great. But the thing I remember the most is how Mom and Dad always had to struggle. I wanted a more secure future for myself."

Without the brothers and sisters, it was so much like his philosophy, Jake noted. But had she taken the criminal route to achieve her financial success? He wanted to know more. "And you grew up in?"

"Washington. Daddy is a plumber and Mom does office work. They were so impressed when I was accepted at Johns Hopkins. At first I studied languages because I thought I'd become a translator, but once I was more or less fluent I sort of lost interest. But the languages are useful on these trips."

Jake closed his eyes and imagined Nora's family. Happy. He could tell that. She might believe that money was what was most important to her, but he knew better. When the right man came along, she wouldn't care what his bank account looked like.

That was what he must try to remember instead of how wide her eyes had grown when he'd kissed her. . . .

Something was crawling up his face and Jake shot out his hand as he opened his eyes. He looked up into Nora's eyes, startled by his grip on her wrist. He realized she was holding a daisy that she'd been using to tickle his face.

"You fell asleep." Her words were soft. Her eyes held a million promises. He raised his other hand to the back of her head and drew her to him. Her eyes grew darker, and she freed her captured hand to touch his hair just as their lips met. He had promised himself one slow, sweet kiss but the second they touched he lost control. His lips plundered hers as he pulled her on top of him, opening his thighs so she could nestle between them and feel his desire. She opened her lips and he explored her mouth. Her hands were running down his back and under his shirt against his hot skin.

"Jake," she gasped as she tore her mouth free.

He started to pull her back to him and then restrained himself. He wasn't used to being so overpowered. He should stop, but he couldn't push her away from him. He kept his eyes closed as she raised herself, and tried to even his breathing, tried to think of anything but how much he wanted her. He pictured a warehouse of identical cartons that had to be searched.

"Jake." Now her voice was questioning, and he felt able to look at her without jumping her—as he'd so rashly promised earlier.

Nora was smiling at him strangely and held out a hand as she stood up. "I did promise to show you how to do *everything* on a bus, didn't I?"

Hardly believing her words, afraid he was getting himself into a situation that was far beyond his control, he followed her into the bus. When he looked around, trying to figure out how, Nora blushed and pointed to the front seat. "If we just push the seat back a little . . ."

Before she could change her mind, Jake sat down and boldly pulled Nora atop him so that she straddled him. Jake held her tightly to him and kissed her. God, she was so soft and sweet. He couldn't get enough of her. He kissed her again and again. Finally, to get some breath into his air-starved lungs, he cradled her face between his hands. Nora's beautiful face was filled with passion. Then she smiled wickedly and began to unbutton his shirt, exploring the exposed flesh with her lips.

"Uh, Nora—" Her lips had captured one of his nipples and his hand tightened around her hips. "Nora, have you done *this* before on a bus?"

Nora raised her flushed face, and he seized the opportunity to grab her shoulders and hold her away from him.

"No, I never have, but this seems like a good opportunity to expand our horizons," she quoted his earlier words. "Don't you want to?" she asked innocently as her hands managed to find an infinitesimal space between their bodies to stroke his erection. He heard the sound of a zipper and then felt Nora's questing fingers.

He thought he should stop her, be the sane one since Nora had clearly lost her senses, but her touch was too erotic. "Of course I wanted to from the first time I kissed you, but I can't promise you anything," he managed to gasp out. When had he lost control of this seduction?

"I don't want any promises."

Jake wanted to demand why not but he was about to explode any second, and he wanted Nora along with him. Jake stilled her movements, pushed the movable armrest up between the seats, creating more space for them, and lowered her to a reclining position. Then he began *his* seduction. He heard her moan as his hands caressed her breasts through the pink lace of her lingerie, his thumbs playing with the hard peaks. He explored the soft skin that was now straining against the confines of the lace with his mouth. She was sprawled across his lap, and he wanted a week to feast on her.

With one hand he slid a strap down her smooth shoulder while his other hand traveled up the back of her thigh. As his lips and tongue tasted her sweet skin, he teasingly traced the lines of her inner thighs without touching the vee in between.

"Jake," Nora demanded. "Jake, please . . ."

"What do you want?"

"I want you to touch me."

Jake moved to caress the other breast with his mouth and this time, when he brushed his hand up Nora's leg, he kept going until he met her liquid warmth, finding and stroking her.

"Jake . . . now . . . I can't hold back." Nora was struggling out of his grasp and righted herself over him. He kissed her lips, lightly then hard, while his hand explored her firm buttocks, then followed the lines of the lace teddy that was still covering her. "It has clips," Nora gasped, and when her meaning sank in, he had her free and then was inside her.

"Perfect." Jake almost didn't recognize the rasp of his own voice as Nora sheathed him and began to gently move against him. He explored the slender column of her throat with his mouth, gripping his hands around her hips to help her movements. She felt so good and welcoming that he didn't ever want making love to Nora to end.

But every time she lifted herself, and then let him enter her again, the need to have more and more built until he was thrusting forward, pulling her down faster and faster until he felt rather than heard her gasp. He thrust forward again, and all control was lost.

He was cradling her head against his shoulder as reality began to return. He ran a hand along her arm and tilted her face toward him. He was gratified to see a bemused expression, and then she smiled.

"If that's what you can do on a bus, Jake Collins, I'd hate to imagine what you can do in a bed."

NORA WISHED SHE AND JAKE could have stayed together longer. She'd been expecting great sex from Jake

Collins—and had gotten it—but she was afraid she was in over her head. She'd wanted him as she'd wanted no other man, and she'd thought only to scratch her itch. But like with so many other bites, that only made it worse.

She could hardly believe her daring—suggesting they make love on the bus. She'd never be able to look at that seat again without blushing!

It had felt liberating to do exactly what she wanted, for once, damn the consequences. To lose control.

It was too late for regrets, she told herself firmly as Jake drove the bus along the highway back to the hotel. *He's a great lover and if you're lucky, he'll remain your lover for the rest of the tour. But that'll be it.*

But a part of her didn't want whatever it was between them to end. And she realized that this stupidly optimistic part of herself was gambling on him feeling the same way. "Wait and see," she muttered.

"What did you say?"

Oh, I was just planning on how to make you fall in love with me so that you won't say goodbye. She couldn't say those things because that was exactly what Jake would expect. She would have to play the game by his rules and cheat whenever possible, if she hoped to win. She refused to even think about whether he was on this trip to investigate her . . . and whether his thrilling lovemaking was part of it. He'd wanted her. She would use that to her advantage, no matter what his motives were. Tearing her gaze away from him she spotted a stranded motorist up ahead. "I said we should stop and see if they need help."

Jake didn't say anything, but he signaled and pulled the bus over to the side of the road just ahead of the car. "Don't get off the bus, Nora. We'll see what they want first."

Jake opened the front door and Nora stood on the bottom step as a man made his way toward them.

"Bonjour, madame, monsieur," he began in French and proceeded to explain how his car had stopped for no reason that he could discern and could he please have a lift to the nearest service station.

"Ask him where his friend inside the car is from," Jake ordered.

Nora turned to him in puzzlement. "What are you talking about?"

"Just ask."

Nora did and told Jake the answer. "His friend lives in Quebec City like he does."

"Hold on," Jake commanded and shot the bus forward, practically knocking the stranded motorist off his feet. Nora grabbed the rail at the front of the bus, swaying close to the still-open door.

"Jake!" she screamed.

Jake swerved the bus in the opposite direction so that she fell inside the bus and the door closed. "Have you lost your mind?" she demanded.

The bus backfired, and Nora braced herself against pitching forward again, but nothing happened. The bus backfired a second time. As the horrible truth dawned on her, she managed to choke out the words, "They're shooting at us!"

10

Environmentally friendly. Unlike air travel, our motor-coach tours pass by scenic wonders, enabling travelers to marvel at nature firsthand. The National Tour Association's recent research study determined that a motor coach carrying forty passengers emits 9.1 grams of carbon monoxide per mile. That's 747 percent less carbon monoxide per mile by motor coach than by car! Buses, an environmentally friendly way to travel.

NORA HIT the hard rubber of the floor just as she felt a hot buzz across the top of her head and heard glass shatter.

"Nora, are you all right?" Jake demanded.

"Someone's shooting at us!"

The bus swerved again, the force throwing Nora across the aisle where she hit her head against a seat. "Ouch. Damn it, will you tell me when you're about to play Evel Knievel in a bus uniform so I can hold on to a nonmoving object?" She pulled herself to her feet and, when she wasn't sent flying like a human cannnonball, peered out the window.

"Good to know your acerbic tongue is still working. But where is Miss Merry Sunshine?"

"She disappears as soon as someone tries to kill me. Jake, those were bullets, weren't they?"

"Why else would I be pushing this bus to qualify for the Indianapolis 500?"

In her shock, Nora hadn't been aware of anything other than the pounding of her heart but now she realized the motor coach was literally hurtling down the road, swinging madly from side to side. Through the rearview mirror she saw the same mustard-colored car following them. "Faster."

"We can't go fast enough to lose them. And all they need to do is shoot out a couple of tires and the accident will be so bad that the investigators will never figure out the cause." The bus engine screamed in complaint as Jake overtook a small sedan and then pulled closely in front of it. To Nora, the blasting horn from the outraged driver sounded much better than the crack of gunfire.

"That will buy us a few minutes. These guys don't want to shoot at us with an audience."

"What about when we stop the bus and get off?"

"We're vulnerable."

For several minutes Nora could only look back and forth between the reflection of the mustard-colored car and the angry sedan, while she tried to absorb the implications of what was happening. She and Jake were in danger—that was blatantly obvious—but why? Jake knew—she'd bet every penny she was investing in her scheme and its profits on that—but this was not the time for questions. They needed to lose their pursuers.

The sedan had managed to break away and was successfully overtaking them. In fine Gallic form, the driver shook an angry fist at them—if it hadn't been for the men with the guns, Nora would have worried. Instead, she giggled.

Jake glanced sharply at her. "Are you sure you weren't hit?"

"No. I was just wondering who was more dangerous to us—Montreal drivers or hit men. I wouldn't want to meet our angry Frenchman the next time I'm out for a pleasant ride in the country. Of course," she added hysterically, "that's what we were doing—taking a pleasant ride in the country before someone shot at us—"

"Nora, take slow deep breaths." Jake waited until he could hear her performing the relaxation exercise. "We'll get out of this, and someday you'll have a wild tale to tell your grandchildren."

"Sure. I'll explain that we simply hid the bus and— That's it! Quick, can you get us far enough ahead so that they lose sight of us around the turns?"

"You need to take some more deep breaths. In...out."

"I want to keep breathing, period. I know this road and I know where to hide the bus. Just step on it!"

She scrambled to the rear of the bus and dragged a box back up to the front.

"What the hell are you doing? This is no time for games."

"We need to get to a point where they can't see us turn off. This—" Nora held up her bag of bingo balls "—will do the trick." She climbed on the seat behind Jake and pulled open his window. "For once, please don't make any sudden turns. I don't want to be splattered all over the road." Twisting and turning, she wriggled until she was halfway out the window. With the wind attacking her face, she suddenly felt airborne and kicked out with her feet to get a firmer hold. Jake's groan told her she'd connected with him; his arm around her waist held her still and made her feel secure.

"For God's sake, be careful." Jake's tone wasn't as steady as his arm.

Nora leaned out as far as she could, holding the bag of bingo balls. "Under the B—bye-bye!" she yelled and overturned the bag. The balls began their furious race toward the mustard car. The driver realized what was happening and swerved, but the suddenly lethal bingo balls rolled relentlessly on, under the wheels of the car, sending it out of control into a ditch.

"Yes!" Nora pumped her hand up and teetered precariously over the road until Jake hauled her back inside. She ended up in an inelegant but happy pile on the floor. "I did it."

Jake checked the mirror. "They're gone, now what?"

Nora scrambled up and pointed. "There, up ahead, turn at the sign."

In his rearview mirror Jake saw their pursuers hadn't made it around the corner yet. With his bad luck, it wouldn't take the villains long to get their car out of the ditch. In a mad swing he turned the bus fast; it swayed and then righted itself onto the small road.

"Damn!" Nora got up from the floor. "Jake Collins, I'm going to be black-and-blue from your crazy driving." She peered out. "They're not behind us."

"No. But it won't take them long to figure out we turned off. Where are we heading?"

"There. Saint Joseph's Oratory."

"A church?" As the large dome came into view, Jake offered up his own prayer to be delivered from foolishly optimistic women. "We're trapped."

"Look around you. What do you see?"

"A parking lot full of cars and— You're a genius!" The large parking area, made to accommodate the scores of worshipers and tourists who visited every day, was full of buses. "We're going to hide our bus in plain sight with our fellow road nomads."

Jake pulled the Merry Travelers caravan into a spot surrounded by identical buses. A few coaches owned and operated by large tour companies had can't-miss colors, but the charter buses were an anonymous breed. Jake and Nora exited and took down the Merry Travelers banners. With all the pink off the bus, it blended in perfectly. After shoving the signs under one of the seats, Jake grabbed Nora and kissed her.

When the long kiss ended he kept his arms around her, hugging her tightly to him. "Are you sure you're all right?"

Nora muttered something into his shirt. He loosened his hold so that she could talk. "I'm scared. Who were those men and why were they shooting at us? How did you know?"

Nora's color had disappeared, her voice quavered. Reaction was setting in. Taking her cold hand, Jake pulled her along. "Let's mingle with the crowd. Tell me about this place." He needed time to decide what to tell her.

In a monotone, Nora did as he'd instructed. "It's the world's largest pilgrimage center devoted to St. Joseph, the patron saint of Canada. The Italian-Renaissance style dome is one of the largest in the world. The original chapel was built in 1904, but Brother André of the Congrégation de Saint-Croix...." Jake let Nora's automatic recitation wash over him while he scanned the crowds. He didn't see anyone he recognized but knew it wouldn't take Lucci's men long to figure out where they were. He and Nora were safe for now, but since the bad guys had made a move, they'd want to finish the game—quickly.

"How did you know those men weren't stranded motorists?" Nora had maneuvered them into a group of sight-seers. She smiled at him weakly. "Thanks for letting me go on automatic. I'm better now."

"I really wanted to know that the shrine, at 263 meters above sea level, is the highest point in Montreal."

"How did you know they were the bad guys?" she repeated.

"The car had New York licence plates."

"So?"

"Why did he have a Québecois accent if he was from New York?"

"He could have been in his friend's car."

"Then why didn't he speak English? We're obviously not Quebecers. That made me suspicious. If they hadn't reacted I would have phoned for help at the nearest service station. They wanted to catch us off guard."

"I could have rolled off the bus with all that maneuvering."

"I'd have rescued you, Nora." Jake's fierce expression held her motionless, until she saw the tour group had abandoned them.

"I believe you would, Jake Collins. You're a good man." He moved closer, and she continued quickly, "Let's catch up with our tourists."

"It feels like I'm spending all my time in the midst of groups, having my photo taken and being knocked over by large lethal handbags."

"You made a joke!" At Jake's scowl Nora smiled and hugged her joy close inside. Jake might not admit it, but he was not as tough and uncaring as he acted. And he liked her. Okay, she conceded, a lot of the attraction was sexual, but he did like her. She could make him laugh. Anything was possible. . . .

"Tell me," she insisted again, when Jake didn't say anything. One second they were so close, and the next he shut down.

"Why were those men shooting at us? What could they have wanted? What's going on?" Nora could hear the hysterical note in her voice and her body began to shake. She stopped walking with the crowd and wrapped her arms tightly around herself. "How did you know?"

"Nora, damn..." Jake stopped and stared at her pale face but made no move toward her. He wanted to believe in her and tell her everything—about Bruce Davis, Lucci's men, the smuggling—but he couldn't.

The impromptu picnic in a secluded spot. Nora could have set him up.

Then why hadn't he been ambushed while Nora had been distracting him? the part of him that wanted to believe her argued. Because it was supposed to look like an accident, cold logic answered. That's why they'd stopped him on the road.

Nora was shivering—in reaction to the plans having gone awry and having been placed in danger? Lucci's men, after all, had been prepared to kill her, as well. That fact would be enough to send anyone into shock.

"Jake, please, what's going on?" Nora repeated.

He ignored the tremulousness of her words and the fear in her eyes. In his coldest voice he asked, "Why don't you tell me what you and Zachary Buch are up to?"

"Oh!" Nora dropped her eyes to the ground but that didn't hide her guilty flush, Jake noted with grim satisfaction. Seconds passed, but he knew silence was an effective interrogation technique.

"I... I can't tell you."

"Nora, I can help you get out of this if you tell me the truth." He reached out to take her hands but she backed away.

"This afternoon...when we, we... How could you! You were using me!" She raised her stricken face. "Weren't you?" She prayed he'd deny it.

Jake's silence confirmed the worst. She'd been foolishly hoping . . . when it had all been an act.

She turned and walked away from him. He didn't follow. She ignored the fact that she'd been using him in a similar manner. She was the offended party, here. She wasn't spying on anyone! People weren't shooting because of her! Lost in her misery she passed through the crowd, trying to hold back tears. She heard her name being called and, hoping it was Jake, turned to see Steve, another Merry Travelers escort, waving at her. Wanting to get as far away from Jake as possible, she hurried over to him.

"Nora, I thought that was you. How's the trip?"

Steve was so nice and uncomplicated, Nora mused. And really great looking, with wavy blond hair, green eyes and a chiseled chin. Why couldn't she fall for him? She wished Jake could see her with him and be jealous—most men were usually intimidated by Steve's looks. Unfortunately, Jake would be far too confident of his own appeal to fall for such an obvious ploy. "You managed to duck your groupies?" she asked, looking around for the clutch of females that were always to be found around Steve. "Has your group finished the tour?"

"Believe it or not, I have a male-only group. Eternal Water Buffaloes, or some such thing." Steve looked her over carefully—she must look worse than she did in her nightmare-in-pink outfit—but he refrained from asking questions. "I was just collecting the last of the stragglers. Do you need a lift back to Montreal?"

"Yes. Thanks, Steve," Nora said gratefully and together they went to the bus. At the sight of the blaring Merry Travelers sign, she quashed a momentary doubt.

Mr. Jake Collins had gotten himself into this mess. He could damn well get himself out.

"G TWELVE. Under the G, number twelve," Nora said, remembering the very different use she'd put bingo balls to yesterday, as the bus trekked along the Trans-Canada Highway toward Quebec City.

"Bingo!" cried out Alicia Hall.

"Darn, she always wins. She must cheat," Molly complained.

"We know she cheats on Harold Anderson," Holly responded as she packed up her card and returned it to Nora. "I wouldn't be surprised to hear what other 'no good' she's up to. Here you are, Nora, dear. Bus bingo is always one of the highlights of my tours. But the balls are rather unusual. What happened?"

"There was an...accident. I used nail polish to paint numbers onto marbles last night."

"Last night, in your room? Alone?"

"Yes."

From Nora's grim tone, Molly and Holly didn't need to wonder what had happened to Jake.

"He abandoned her after they were doing so well!" Molly groused.

"I'm sure he had to chase the diamond smugglers."

"Men! They've always got their priorities screwed up!"

Collecting the last of the bingo cards, Nora observed the animated discussion between the two matchmakers but didn't have the energy to rebuke them. After all, she'd had very similar ideas only yesterday.

She was hurt and confused and scared. Steve had been a treasure, letting Nora attach herself to his group, entertaining her, distracting her. She'd been more than a little tipsy when she'd defiantly created new bingo balls in her hotel room. Alone.

There'd been no apologetic Jake to greet her as she'd secretly hoped.

Instead, she'd painted numbers on marbles, each representing a different torture created especially for Mr. Collins.

It was only when, trying to get to sleep, she realized that if Jake Collins had been hired by Bruce Davis to investigate her, who had shot at them?

And why?

11

Experience the delights of yesterday! All of our tours include stops at historic sights, many of which include tableaux of what life was like 100, 200, 300 years ago.

JACQUES WAS A Quebec City tourist trap. Picnic tables were set up in long rows and crowded with eager sightseers. Jacques, a restaurant, entertainment center, bar and much-loved bus stop, offered hourly exhibitions of French-Canadian folk dancing and derring-do by lumberjacks throwing tree trunks. The crowd loved it.

Jake hated it.

He'd hated most of the past day and a half, ever since Nora had disappeared at St. Joseph's. He'd spent several hours searching for her, fearing that Lucci's men had taken her against her will; or worse, that she'd gone willingly. When he'd covered every inch of the church, including the confessionals, he'd returned to the hotel. There, Molly and Holly had disapprovingly told him that Nora had gone out with another tour group.

Feeling like a fool, he'd wanted to find her, to force the truth from her, but had not. Instead, he'd searched the rooms he'd been unable to get to earlier, but other than Holly's fondness for purple lingerie, he'd learned nothing new.

Nora had ignored him throughout the drive to Quebec City, and with Bruce Davis having joined the group—so he could experience one of his own tours, he'd claimed—Jake hadn't even been able to get Nora alone at a coffee stop. Thankfully, Bruce had found tacky Jacques beyond the call of duty and hadn't joined them.

The crowd roared as an ax hurtled through the air and landed with deadly accuracy on the bull's-eye. Despite the early-morning trip to Quebec City, the Merry Travelers were living it up. At one point Nora had had an intimate discussion with Bruce Davis and then scowled at Jake, when she'd seen him watching her. Nora had kept herself surrounded so that he hadn't been able to talk to her without creating a scene. Not that he knew what he wanted to say.

Yes, he did. He wanted to tell her the truth about himself and learn she wasn't involved. That she was innocent. He'd thought he'd trained himself not to be vulnerable, but Nora had turned everything on end. He knew better, but still he wanted her to be innocent.

And when he discovered she wasn't, what then?

Jake felt the beginnings of a headache as the show ended and space was made for a dance floor. He saw Holly heading purposefully toward him. Molly had already dragged him onto the floor for a jig. With footwork that Molly would have loved to see earlier, he moved between the couples and tables and through a door marked Staff. He wasn't a coward, he assured himself, just prudent.

He was in the staff coatroom. Deciding his throbbing head deserved a few moments' respite he sat on the floor, leaning his head against a wall.

"Did you get the information?" He heard the muffled question through the wall.

Instantly alert, Jake realized the corridor was on the other side of the coatroom. Jacques, or whoever owned this monstrosity, having spent all of his money on the tacky decor, hadn't bothered building strong walls between the rooms. Pressing his ear against the thin partition, he listened. He could make out two voices—a man's and a woman's.

"You're pushing too fast," the woman said. "He's already suspicious."

"We don't have a lot of time. We need to move now. Or are you getting cold feet?"

"No, it's just that there have been a lot of . . . complications." She was becoming angry. "Jake knows—"

"He's your job."

"I know. I'll take care of him. Soon."

There were a few more hushed whispers that Jake couldn't make out and then the sound of fading footsteps.

He hadn't been able to recognize the man's voice but he knew the woman. It was Nora.

He held his now pounding head in his hands, asking himself why he'd expected anything different. He'd learned the opposite long ago.

Lethargy held him captive a few minutes longer, as he tried to plod through his options. Finally, he rose and made his way to the front of the club where the cashier was able to find him some aspirin. He swallowed three, dry, and went to find Nora. It was past time for a confrontation.

Her back was to him as she spoke animatedly to Molly and Holly. He caught her by the waist and turned her around while smiling at the duo. "Excuse us, ladies, but I have a sudden need to dance with Nora."

The two waved him off, and he pulled Nora with him. As he circled her waist and held her small hand in his, he discovered he was furiously angry. He didn't look at her, but moved them around the floor until they were beside the exit.

As if realizing his intent, Nora tried to push herself away from him. "Let go of me!" she demanded, but couldn't break his grip. "I don't want anything to do with you—"

"But you're going to take *care* of me," he crooned into her ear. "Isn't that what the seduction was all about?"

"How dare you insult *me* when you're the one who's spying!" She practically hissed the words at him.

Jake lost the last tenuous threads of control. He pulled Nora out the exit into the alley and whirled her to face him. He felt his anger flush his face and his mouth harden into a thin line.

Nora's eyes glittered with what he knew was rage as she stubbornly raised her chin. Her breath was coming in labored gasps, drawing his eyes to the rise and fall of her breasts. He realized his headache had disappeared and that he was incredibly aroused.

"I overheard you just now." Jake tried to focus on the needs of the job and not his body. "Who were you talking to?"

"No." Nora poked a finger into his chest. He stepped back but she followed. "You tell me what's going on. I'm tired of your snooping."

He was back up against the outside wall of Jacques, with Nora only inches away, each trying to stare the other down. "To hell with it," Jake muttered as he pulled her to him by the elbows and kissed her. With a muffled gasp she responded passionately, opening her mouth, pressing herself against him.

The blood pounded through his body. He wasn't capable of thought, only of feeling. And of knowing there was only one woman he wanted. Hungrily he ran his hands down Nora's back, exploring her soft contours, and felt her shiver. This excited him even more and he raised his head, searching for someplace where they could—

Nora stumbled back when Jake abruptly pushed her away from him, and tried to pull all of her senses together.

She'd taken the coward's way out yesterday, running away from Jake and avoiding him ever since. She couldn't pretend anymore.

"You're right, I've been lying to you."

At Nora's soft-spoken words, Jake felt a hit to the gut. He had been right, damn it. Why was he always right?

Nora just couldn't keep up the pretense any longer. She'd never been good with secrets; she'd been wrong to think she could pull it off now. "Bruce sent you to spy on me, I understand that, but what about the gunmen? And Mrs. Reid's attacker? That can't be connected to me. No charter company is worth that!"

Jake stared at her in confusion. "What are you talking about? I'm not spying for Bruce Davis."

"Then who are you working for?" Worry crossed Nora's face. "Oh, my God. You're a criminal. I'm involved with a criminal!" Her voice rose and she began to pace. "I can't believe this. What is it, what are you involved in? Why did your accomplices keep shooting at us?"

"They only shot twice."

"Which is twice too often!"

"Damn it, Nora, they're not my accomplices! They're criminals."

Nora whirled on him, eyes blazing. "And I suppose you're a good guy—sneaking around hotel corridors, following us...."

"Yes."

"Prove it," she commanded.

Jake held his head; his headache had returned—extrastrength. He took slow, deep breaths. How had this woman put him on the defensive? He was a good guy;

she was the one who was out to get him. "How were you going to 'take care of' me?" he asked, his voice cold.

Nora shivered at the ice in his eyes, then dropped her gaze, embarrassed. She'd had decidedly...lustful ideas in mind when she'd made that claim, and *that* she wouldn't admit to Jake Collins even if her life depended upon it.

"Were you going to take me to bed again—or show me some other interesting positions on the bus?" he demanded with contempt.

Nora blazed. "How dare you, you . . . you—"

"Spy?"

"Yes!" She poked him in the chest. "I had sex with you because I wanted to, because I couldn't help myself— not for some underhanded reason like getting information out of you." That was true. The last thing she was capable of when Jake kissed her was any kind of rational thought. He simply overwhelmed her.

Jake stared at her for a long moment, his face so still she would have sworn he was carved out of rock. Which was just her luck, Nora concluded. She was involved in the most sexually fulfilling relationship of her life and the man cared absolutely nothing for her.

"I couldn't help myself, either," Jake finally said.

All the breath that Nora hadn't realized she was holding rushed out of her. "You couldn't?" she asked hopefully.

"No. All I wanted was to touch you."

"Oh." She shouldn't feel so happy, but Nora glowed. She wanted to dance up and down the alleyway. Then reality intruded; he was still a spy. "If Bruce didn't send you to investigate me, then who did?"

Jake grew uneasy. "Why would anyone want to investigate *you?*" What could Nora be involved in? Maybe she was part of the smuggling ring and doing her best to confuse him.

"Why are you spying?" Her color high, she glared at him.

"I'm not a spy," he said smoothly.

Nora stomped her foot. "Oh, this is ridiculous! I'm *not* guilty of anything."

"You have a guilty conscience." Jake cupped her face in his hand and made her look at him. He found Nora Stevens so easy to read. "Tell me."

All the fight went out of Nora. She wanted nothing more than to trust Jake. She opened her mouth, closed it and decided. They had to be honest with each other at some point. It might as well be now. "I'm leaving Merry Travelers to open up my own tour company." At Jake's less-than-impressive response to her declaration, Nora hurried on. "I'll be competing directly against Bruce and will be picking up a lot of overseas business he's let slide."

"It's an expensive proposition," Jake said wearily. Her answer made a lot of sense, but starting a business like that took a lot of money—money she could be getting from Lucci.

"That's why I have a backer . . . who wants to remain anonymous," she added, at Jake's darkening look. "Jake, please—" she touched his arms, her face desperate "—I haven't done anything wrong—not nice, maybe—but please don't tell Bruce. I was planning to hand in my resignation after two more trips, but I'll do it at the end of this one if you like."

"So that's what all your meetings with every Peter, Walter and busboy have been about. You've been busy setting up your own contacts."

"Yes. Oh, Jake, I'm good at this business and Bruce is wasting opportunities that I plan to take advantage of."

"And this backer, how does he have the money?" Jake wished Nora would tell him everything. Maybe he could help her. "Honey, if he's blackmailing you into anything . . ."

"Oh, no, Jake, it was all my idea. You see, my partner won the lottery."

The answer was so incredible it had to be true. "Your silent partner won the lottery and decided to invest in a fledgling bus tour company?"

At Nora's solemn nod, Jake laughed. This woman was truly crazy. That had to be why he liked her so much. He'd check into her story immediately, but there was a good chance she was telling the truth. He grinned.

Nora stared at him, puzzled. What the devil did he have to be so happy about? "Now you tell me, Jake Collins, who are you, really?"

Jake considered what to tell her. It would be so easy to concoct a feasible lie; it was what he was trained to do. "I'm a special agent with U.S. Customs." It felt good telling the truth about himself to Nora. He'd worry about that later.

"What?" Never in her wildest fantasies had she thought of anything like that! "You're a special agent with the government?"

"Yes."

"But why are you here?"

"Because Merry Travelers is involved in a major smuggling operation."

"Smuggling? Smuggling what?"

Jake weighed his words carefully. "We're not sure. I'm here to find out and stop it."

"But I don't understand. What makes you think Merry Travelers is involved in something illegal?"

Jake sighed. "Ever since Bruce Davis took control of his mother's company it's been losing money, but his life-style has become more and more extravagant. And his bank accounts are too healthy."

"But that doesn't mean anything! Mrs. Davis is a wealthy woman and she could be lending her son money." Nora refused to believe what Jake was claiming. It was too outrageous!

"True, but Bruce does have some rather unsavory friends, in particular some close associates he shares with Angelo Lucci."

"The Mob boss?"

"Exactly."

Nora fixed him a level stare. "What else do you have?"

"Isn't that enough?"

"No," she stated calmly. "Bruce may have some . . . unusual acquaintances but that doesn't mean he's a criminal."

"You're right. We have a tip, from a very reliable source, that Lucci's family is underwriting Davis's business because of what is crossing the U.S.-Canada border on his buses."

"But *what* is it?"

"That's the problem. We can't figure out *what* is being transported."

"So why haven't you pulled over one of the buses when it crosses the border and searched it?"

"Because we might pull over a bus that's empty and thereby warn the Lucci family that we're on to them."

"So you're here undercover."

"Yes. Before we set up a trap, we need to know how to bait it."

"And you suspect everything and everyone—including me," Nora said.

"Yes."

"I can't believe this. It's ridiculous! I've been doing these runs for years and I haven't seen anything unusual. Can't your source be wrong?" Nora pleaded.

"No. Our source is impeccable."

"Why did you tell me this? Aren't I a suspect?" Hope flared in her eyes.

"I'm trusting you . . . for now."

"Well, you're wrong."

"About trusting you?"

"Of course not. I think you're wrong about Merry Travelers and I'll help you to prove how wrong you are. I know all these people." There had to be some mistake. She wasn't naive enough to expect the guilty party to be wearing shiny pinstripe suits and carry violin cases, but she just couldn't believe that one of *her* passengers was a smuggler for the Mafia. Of course, she couldn't say the same for Bruce Davis. And these money-losing trips had been worrying her for some time. It was just that, for most of that time, she'd been afraid Bruce had been on to her plans and would sabotage them.

Decided, she faced Jake. "So you're here to spy on all of us and figure out what's going on. That night I thought I heard someone in the Chance brothers' room, that was you?"

"Yes. But I didn't find anything."

"Have you been through my room?"

"No," he lied.

"You mean not yet." When Jake looked like he was about to make excuses, she brushed it aside and continued. "So who are your suspects?"

"As you said, everyone. I'm here to watch and narrow down the field." The background checks on the passengers should be in his hands soon. Because of the nature of the industry, it was impossible to get the final passenger list until after the tour had left—there was always the possibility of a last minute addition or cancellation. Plus he needed to discover who Nora's backer was. Her plans to open up her own tour company sounded good but gave her ample reason to need money. Nora might have believed that her supposed honesty would throw him off the track, but that wouldn't fool him. She ran this route more often than any of the other escorts.

"But what about the gunmen yesterday?" Nora returned to the topic that had her scared.

"I recognized one as Lucci's man, a careless move on his part. Obviously he was expecting to dispose of us quickly."

"Dispose?" Nora echoed weakly.

"It's not a game, Nora. These men are serious and they've figured out who I am. Mrs. Reid's attack was only a distraction, to keep my attention occupied. Since that didn't work, they've turned serious. They've already put one of our agents into intensive care.

"Oh."

Jake found himself wanting to tell Nora about E.J. "She and I were partners on several cases. She's one of the best agents I know. She's always able to gather more information by listening to people for an hour than I'm able to dig up in a week of legwork."

"What happened?" Nora wasn't sure if she really wanted to know, but she needed to if she was to help Jake and her passengers.

"She infiltrated Merry Travelers as a temporary office worker six months ago. You must have met her."

She had indeed, Nora thought sourly. The beautiful redhead had been efficient, courteous and helpful. The curious had wondered whether she might be Bruce

Davis's latest girlfriend but soon realized she was too smart for that.

"But Emma left to go take care of sick aunt."

"No, that's the story we put out. E.J. was beaten— so badly it didn't look like she was going to make it. She wouldn't have if some wino hadn't found her in a dumpster and had the decency to get help."

"I'm sorry. You must care for her a great deal."

"She's a good agent so I asked to be assigned to this case."

"I see." Nora saw a great deal, including how Jake refused to admit how much he cared for a friend. Did he love her?

"What did she uncover?" she asked instead.

"Most of what I've told you. There are two sets of books. In the real version, Merry Travelers is operating at a loss but Bruce Davis isn't worried. The money definitely isn't coming from his mother. E.J. overheard them having a fight about the business. Mrs. Davis is convinced her son is ruining it, but he had E.J. show her the doctored books. Our wiretaps didn't reveal anything.

"The only thing E.J. knew for sure was that this trip, Number 626, is part of it. That's why I'm here."

Nora didn't like the sound of any of this—especially how fondly Jake talked of the woman she'd known as Emma—but she straightened her shoulders and smiled at Jake. "Come on then. You've got me to help you now. I'll be a good partner." She ignored his scowl. "And I'll prove that none of my passengers are involved!"

12

This tour includes incredible variety—from the historic, cultured and cosmopolitan life of Quebec City and Montreal to the rugged man-against-nature-backdrop of the countryside. This land is 3,600 million years old. A land once covered by ice that carved rivers, lakes, valleys and fjords. A land that challenges man and woman.

"YOU'RE DOING IT all wrong!"

Nora turned to see Jake standing behind her. She was sitting on the stone wall, a remnant of the fortifications on the Plains of Abraham, where the General Wolfe had won what was then New France for the British. She'd been chasing members of her seniors gang all morning and was tired. "You spy your way, I'll spy mine."

Jake took off his sunglasses to glare at her. "Discover anything?" he asked sarcastically.

"I spent a ridiculous morning chasing my customers—my friends!" Her frustration level was high. She felt like a cheat, sneaking after people. How did Jake do this for a living?

"I told you you wouldn't like doing this," Jake growled at her. "And if you'd followed my plan and done some of the follow-up on the bios instead of doing what you wanted—" Jake gave up. Nora never listened to his advice. "What happened?"

"Mrs. Reid abandoned her husband at a café where he was joined by the Chance brothers. I left them there and followed Mrs. Reid. She went shopping—children's clothing."

"Did it look like Mr. Reid expected to meet up with the Chances?"

"It looked unplanned but I can't be sure. I bumped into Janet and Alicia in front of the bank but they were heading back to the hotel. That's all I have to report, sir." Nora saluted him.

"Are you mad at me?"

"Mad? Why should I be mad?"

"Because I'm here investigating your passengers, got you shot at and haven't said a word about us after we, I—"

"After I seduced you? That was my one dumb idea."

"After we made love." Jake ignored Nora's words. He'd replayed their lovemaking too frequently when he should have been working. His response to Nora unsettled him. She was probably innocent—unless she was the best actress he'd ever met—but she was trouble. She never obeyed his orders. She insisted that she was right and U.S. Customs wrong. She was going to run straight into trouble and pull him along with her!

Jake tried to think of an approach that would work with her. He watched a young toddler aggressively attack a slight hill and fall. His mother picked up the child and pushed him up the incline. When Nora didn't jump in with anything, he cleared his throat. She looked expectantly at him. "I don't know what to say to you. Thanks for a memorable picnic? I won't be around once the case is closed."

"Why not?"

"My work."

"That's a load of bull. If you wanted you'd make room for the right woman, your work wouldn't interfere."

"I don't want to."

"You're scared." Nora didn't know how she knew, but she was sure she was right. "But that's okay," she said brightly, "I don't have time in my life for a serious relationship, anyway."

"The hell you don't." Jake glowered at her. "You're the kind of woman who goes steady."

"Not anymore," Nora said. "Besides, as soon as I resign from Merry Travelers I'm going to be too busy with my new business. A man, any man, is an unnecessary complication. Maybe that's why I found you so attractive, even after I learned you were a spook—"

"Agent."

"Whatever." She waved a hand. "We're completely incompatible, Jake. Especially because of our work. We're both used to running the show—not compromising. I'd drive you nuts in a week. You'd send me over the edge in less time."

"That's because you refuse to listen to good advice." He glared at her. "You're saying that you don't want anything more than a few good times in bed?" Jake ground the words out.

"Oh, I want a lot more than that," Nora answered, to Jake's relief. She had to want something more between them. All these feelings couldn't be only on his side. She smiled her beautiful smile and Jake felt his heart race as he reached for her. When his lips were a whisper away, she said, "I want a *great* time in bed."

He froze.

"Jake, what's wrong?"

"Nothing." He pushed away from her like she had the plague. What the hell was the matter with him? A beautiful woman was admitting she wanted him for a good time, not a long time. He should be thrilled. The only reason he wasn't, the only reason he was thinking how much he'd like to try for something more was that Nora didn't want to. The thrill of the hunt—that was all. He scowled at her.

"Jake, is it something about the case?"

Nora sounded worried about the stupid case. He wanted to shake her and force her to say she had to see him after the damn case closed. Then he could drop her. Control.

"Did you find out something...something about one of my passengers? Is that what you're not telling me?" Nora demanded.

"No. I haven't learned anything new." But he was learning a lot about himself.

Nora considered him for a moment. "So we keep dogging our Merry Travelers until you discover there's nothing going on?"

"Until someone makes a false move. Come on—" he pulled her up "—let's go spy on someone." And he was going to ignore all the stupid fantasies he'd played out last night. He had a job to do.

Nora walked with him. He could be so infuriating, insisting on doing things his way—she was used to steamrollering over opposition and was finding the experience exhilarating. She didn't know what was bothering Jake, but in a weird kind of way she was having the time of her life. Her bus trip had turned into an intrigue with the bonus of the sexiest man she'd ever met. She was determined to enjoy every second that Jake Collins was around. "I'll help you only if my favorite secret agent buys me an ice-cream cone."

"Customs agent, and— Oh, never mind. It's a deal." Unable to resist, he pulled her close and kissed her.

"Mmm, I like how you deal, officer," she murmured vampishly several breathless moments later. "Can we try plea bargaining next?"

Jake laughed and Nora joined step with him. After he'd bought her the ice cream they headed toward the hotel. This afternoon they were to drive along the rugged Gaspé coast for two days of relaxation at the Manoir Richelieu. It was his last chance to solve the case before the tour was over. And his last few days to spend with Nora.

That thought bothered him more than the idea of not solving the case.

JAKE DIDN'T KNOW what to do. And this unusual occurrence had happened at the most damnable of times. For as long as he could remember he had always had a plan—to study hard and win scholarships, to do even better at college so that he could do something worthwhile with his life. Law enforcement had always attracted him, ever since he was a kid.

Before he joined the special Customs force he'd never been passionate about anything. He'd cared about his mother and a few girlfriends, but nothing could sidetrack him from his goal. He didn't know why or when he'd decided to become a cop. He'd always wanted to be one. His earliest memories of Christmas were of presents that unwrapped to reveal shiny tin badges and blue hats.

Naturally the investigative end of Customs was a little different from the street work he'd imagined from television shows and novels; still, he'd felt a sense of belonging and being needed that had almost overwhelmed him until he'd learned to keep a tight rein on his emotions. But he threw himself into his work, reveling in the challenge, the intricate puzzles, the sheer thrill of slapping the cuffs on the criminal he'd been tracking for weeks.

But he didn't know what to do about Nora. Despite the fact he had no proof, he believed her. Hell, he wasn't even checking into her silent partner because he wanted to trust her. He knew he was behaving like a fool, but that didn't stop him.

He knew the consequences of behaving like a fool— or where blind trust could lead him. He'd trusted his partner, Harry Stanton, even when the facts were pointing to his being on the take. Jake had been wrong and it had almost cost another officer his life. Was he repeating the same mistake?

Jake halted at the cliff edge and stared out at the turbulent waters of the St. Lawrence. The grandeur of the Manoir Richelieu, the popular destination of jazz-age millionaires, still retained its stately allure, the softly rolling lawns made him picture young girls in spring dresses, playing croquet. The large chairs in secluded little groups were made for daydreaming about when steamships eased their way down the river.

The Merry Travelers had arrived late yesterday. His reconnaissance had revealed none of Lucci's men, but they could be biding their time. And he was getting nowhere. The frisky seniors had been inactive last night—exhausted or conserving their strength?—and he had spent several long hours wandering the corridors. Once, he stood in front of Nora's door but then left, calling himself a coward. A professional would have taken advantage but he was afraid of what he would feel. The rational solution was to stop his involvement with Nora. His eyes had been opened, now he just needed to stay alert.

If only it were that easy.

He looked at his watch: 7:30 a.m. The happy campers would soon be up and at 'em, with him dogging their heels. But unlike Rover, he wasn't receiving his reward—the proof of what was going on. Today he was going to follow the Chance brothers again; he hadn't been able to get a hold of Tim's backpack and he planned to today.

Yesterday, before he'd met Nora, he'd checked out Zachary Buch, only to discover he was the most zealous tourist ever sent on a bus tour. Zachary had covered most of the attractions in Quebec City, as if he was on a whirlwind schedule, taking pictures and furiously scribbling notes. Jake couldn't believe anything illegal had transpired under his careful scrutiny, and his frustration had only grown. The trip was nearing its end, and other than bruises to his body and his ego, he had nothing.

Spotting Holly and Molly waving to him from the terrace breakfast tables, he waved back and turned in the opposite direction toward the front doors. Holly and Molly had been at many of the stops he'd covered yesterday. Every time he had spotted one of the dotty dowagers she'd pulled an absurd hat down low and ducked. If he didn't know better he'd have thought they were following him.

Turning the corner he saw Nora and Bruce standing on the front steps. From his vantage point he could see them without being seen himself. He moved in even closer to overhear their words. Nora's voice was angry.

"What you're asking me to do is ridiculous, Bruce!"

"You'd do it if you cared for me," he wheedled softly. "We go back a long way, Nora. It's not like you'd be doing something you didn't want to anyway. I've seen the way you look at him."

"You're nothing better than a pimp!" Nora angrily paced away from Bruce, covering her ears. "I can't believe what I'm hearing!"

Neither could Jake. He'd been so overcome by anger that he'd forgotten about Nora's discussion with the mysterious man and her words: *I'll take care of him.* Could she and Bruce really be a team? Could everything she had said, everything she'd done be a ruse to throw him off Bruce's trail?

He'd been wrong before.

Bruce cupped Nora's elbows and held her to him. "Please?"

"Oh, Bruce." Nora touched his face tenderly and Jake ground his teeth. "Tell me what's going on, I want to help you."

So Nora only wanted to help Bruce. Jake was relieved, but his exultation died when he realized exactly what she was doing. She was trying to warn Bruce. Of all the idiot, stupid things she'd done so far. . . .

He shook the bush he was hiding behind and saw the two of them jump apart like a pair of adulterous lovers caught in the act. He felt as vengeful as the outraged husband. "Good morning," he shouted cheerfully as he made his way from behind the shrub as if he'd been out for a morning walk.

Nora was pale but looked happy to see him. Bruce glared first at Jake, then at her. "Find out," he ordered, "or else you're fired." With a last contemptuous look at Jake, Bruce stalked off.

"I'm having a lousy day and it's not even 8:00 a.m.," Nora began, wishing Jake would hold her and tell her everything would work out. Instead, he scowled at her. Now what was the matter with him? He hadn't come to her room last night. She'd told herself that he was off spying but knew he was avoiding her. Like the first time she'd seen him, his mirrored sunglasses shielded his eyes from her.

She shook off a chill. "Bruce is suspicious of me—he threatened to fire me."

"I'm sure you'll be able to work your magic on him and have him wrapped around your little finger."

"What's wrong? I didn't tell him anything."

"But you would have if I hadn't interrupted." At her flush, he nodded. "And that would have blown any hope I had of catching Bruce Davis or Lucci. There's still a chance they're only suspicious of me—they don't have any evidence. You were about to give it to him."

"Oh, I'm so sorry," Nora pleaded. "It's just that I saw Bruce and thought that maybe if we talked—"

"That he wouldn't turn out to be guilty."

At Nora's damning silence Jake shook his head. "Get this through your pretty head. Bruce Davis is guilty. I'm here on an investigation and not a vacation. You run your silly campers around, I'll figure this out. Now, if you'll excuse me, I have work to do." Jake stomped off.

Nora watched him leave in as much of a fit as Bruce had been in only moments earlier. Jake was right. She would have hurt his case.

Bruce had caught her by surprise, suggesting she get close to Jake to find out why he was on the trip. Oh, Bruce had couched his reasons in pleasant words, claiming he feared a competitor was planning to sabotage his tours. But Nora had realized that she was wrong and Jake was right about Merry Travelers. Bruce was up to his neck in whatever Jake was tracking. That meant some of her passengers were involved, as well.

She felt as if the rose tint had come off her world. She wished she could have thrown herself into Jake's arms, had him comfort her and tell her it would all be fine.

It wouldn't be.

13

Bienvenue! Welcome to the heart of Quebec. The quaint town of Gaspé welcomes you with its warmth and charm. The picturesque storybook houses are nestled over a majestic view of the St. Lawrence. Enjoy real Québecois hospitality!

THE HOUSE WAS SMALL and well kept. Someone spent a lot of time lovingly taking care of the garden. The Chance brothers had wandered through the little Gaspé town so aimlessly that Jake knew they had a definite destination. They had passed by this house three times and now, having ascertained the street was clear of people, practically ran up the walk and inside. The garden offered good cover as Jake made his way to the front window. He was glad that something was finally happening. If he was lucky he might get the opportunity to hit someone—although the person he really wanted to hit was Bruce Davis.

And he would.

Jake peered in the window. The scene before him was enough to make James Bond raise his eyebrows with glee. Tim Chance placed his backpack on the dining table. Jake could almost hear the jangle of keys as his brother removed the heavy key chain from around his neck and unlocked the bag. Tim opened the pack and stepped back with a flourish. It was full of money. Even from the window Jake saw it was Canadian money— in the pleasing brown shade of hundred-dollar bills.

Time slowed as he focused on separate images in the scene like the videographer of a foreign film. John's twitching eyes and the old man's red nose. The man stepped toward the money, touching it reverently. He pulled out a tattered handkerchief, blew his nose vigorously, then eyed the cash again. Tim said something and the old man nodded, shuffling off to another room.

Come on.... Come on, Jake willed. This was it. His palms tingled for the feel of his automatic. He wished he could take them down instead of collecting information.

The old man returned, barely able to carry the box, but he refused John's help as he placed it on the table next to the money and stepped back triumphantly.

What was in it? Jake doubted the old man was into drugs but it could be counterfeit plates or artifacts or jewels or—

Hockey cards! Jake froze as a very pale John opened the box and pulled out hockey cards. There had to be hundreds and hundreds of them.

Tim and John began to sort through the cards, discarding some, chortling over others. The old man counted his money. Jake watched as time and a pair of suspects were slipping away from him. He'd had enough of this.

At the front door his furious pounding led to a sudden rush of activity and the old man calling, "*Attendez.*"

Not waiting, Jake opened the door and marched in. Tim and John froze with hands full of the hockey cards they were stuffing back in the box while the old man straightened—after having shoved his backpack full of cash under the sofa.

"*Monsieur, qu'est-ce que vous voulez?*"

"I want to know what's going on here," Jake demanded in authoritative tones. He walked over to the table and picked up an errant card from the floor—Darryl Sittler, Toronto Maple Leafs. "Why have you been carrying around so much money?"

"I told you he wasn't an ordinary bus driver—that he was after us," Tim hissed to his brother.

But John was made of stronger stuff. "You're too late. Monsieur Leduc has agreed to sell to us. You might as well leave."

"Unless this gentleman has a better offer?" Monsieur Leduc beamed at his uninvited guest.

"You can't! We have a deal."

"Not until I've considered all the offers. What is your price, sir?" The old man had to blow his nose again at this fine example of the free enterprise system at work.

Jake stared at Monsieur Leduc and then the two infuriated Chance brothers. "An offer, yes, but first I want to examine the merchandise," he said carefully, "before I can better these gentlemen."

Tim's fist hit him hard. Jake avoided the follow-up punch in a neat duck and weave so that he was behind Tim and then holding him in a hammerlock.

"Tim, damn it, you'll cost us this deal with your temper." John turned a pleading face to Jake. "Mr. Collins, I must apologize for my brother's foolish actions but he has a...peculiar sense of honor. With your arrival he feels . . . cheated."

Tim squirmed but Jake tightened his hold. "Is that right, Tim, do you feel cheated?"

"I worked for months convincing Monsieur Leduc he wanted to sell and I've given him a fair price. *I* was the one to find him, not you! What lowlife do you work for? Nick from Sporting Way or Wayne at Memories? Well, you can tell them they're too late. Mr. Leduc is selling his collection to Cards by Chance!" Tim's voice had reached a crescendo of outrage. Jake let Tim go and turned to Monsieur Leduc.

"These gentlemen are buying your collection of hockey cards?"

"*Mais oui.* I've collected since I was a little boy, but not until that Monsieur Chance told me about the baseball card that sells for over $450,000 did I think what I had might be worth so much money. Now I have a nice retirement 'nest egg' like they say in the commercials, no? I just didn't know that I was investing when I was kid!" The last words came out on a gasp of laughter as Leduc pulled out his handkerchief to blow his nose and wipe at his wet eyes. He continued to wheeze as he pulled out the backpack and fondled his money.

John pulled his short self to full height. "I hope you will forgive my brother, but this time Cards by Chance has won. I didn't believe Tim when he said we had to sneak here under the cover of a bus tour to fool the competition—Tim, forgive me, I'll believe you from now on—but we've won. And the publicity we'll receive from this collection will put us on the cover of all the collectors' magazines, hell even some of the sports magazines. Cards by Chance is going to be known from coast to coast. You're out of luck, so get out." John pointed to the door dramatically and then looked at Jake hopefully.

Jake was happy to comply because he realized he had broken in on a legal transaction. Cards by Chance was a well-established sports memorabilia shop in Georgetown he'd passed by often. He would let Tim and John believe he was a spy for the competition. It was better than what he'd call himself.

TIRED OF FOLLOWING her mischievous passengers, and thoroughly depressed by Bruce's actions, Nora decided to find Jake. She wanted him to reassure her, but more important, she just wanted a chance to be with him. Her mother had always said subtlety didn't work. "If you want something you have to go after it and let intentions be known to scare off the competition." So far, she had applied this maxim to her professional life; it was time to use it in her personal life. And she didn't have a lot of time with Jake. She wanted to make the most of it. An affair wasn't much if they only did it once! That would be a one-night stand, and she wasn't that kind of girl. She had a reputation to uphold—even if she had to drag Jake kicking and screaming into bed!

It had been surprisingly easy to follow Jake following the Chance brothers. Obviously Jake was worried or he would have spotted her immediately. She was just thinking about going into the house as well when Jake ran out as if his worst nightmare was inside. Nora waited at the front gate.

He stopped in front of her, smiling that odd, crooked smile of confidence and vulnerability. "Following me, Nora?"

"Yes."

"Come on, then." He placed his arm around her shoulder. "I made a fool of myself in there. I might as well listen to what you have to say."

"I'm not sure I like what you're saying but I'll ignore it." It was nice walking along the quiet street with Jake, like they were a couple.

"I discovered the Chance brothers' guilty secret. They're collectors of sports memorabilia, especially bubble gum cards. They're using the tour as a cover to get to the latest find before the competition does."

"See, there's probably a perfectly reasonable explanation for everything."

Was she wrong to want him to stop before he got too close? It was time to push. "Everyone? Do you have any innocent secrets you're keeping from me?"

"No." She was afraid that her face was betraying her again. He seemed in a receptive mood; maybe now was the time to seduce him.

They continued in silence along the winding street, until the houses ended and the roadway turned into more of a walking path. Jake directed them off the trail along the shore to where several trees and a hedge offered shelter from the sun and wind. Jake laid out his leather jacket for her to sit on and knelt beside her. The trees hid them from the pathway.

"Jake, I—"

His fingers at her lips cut her off. "Let's not talk." His gaze held hers. She saw his passion but was afraid he wasn't going to do anything. He closed his eyes and said, "I want you more than any other woman."

Jake's lips were on her, hard and possessive, and she was crushed against the earth, his strong body over hers. He was kissing her like he could never have enough of her, but she was willing to give him everything. His hand trailed along the side of her breast, down the curve of her waist and flare of her hip, teasing, tantalizing. As his leg inserted itself between hers, she moaned and moved under him. A small shift of her body put her breast in the path of his roving hand. He captured her breast, outlining her nipple between thumb and forefinger. She gasped.

"Easy, baby, easy. I want to make it so good for you."

"Jake . . . I need . . ."

Jake raised himself on one elbow, the other hand unbuttoning her blouse. His leg continued its erotic movements between hers. Her blouse was open. "Damn, but you have the prettiest underwear." His finger traced the edge of her lace-trimmed cream camisole. "I especially like these pretty bows tying it together." His breath was hot against her skin, burning her, and his wet tongue between her breasts only stoked the fire higher. He brushed his lips against one hard nipple, then the other.

He raised his head to watch the rapid rise and fall of her breasts, which were pushing against the lace keeping her from him. "Let's see how these pretty bows undo." With lips and teeth he pulled at a ribbon, baring her flesh.

"I'm sure I saw them go this way, Holly."

"Jake." Nora pushed at him.

He raised his head from her throat. "What, honey, did I do something you didn't like?" He kissed a different area.

"Oh, stop that— I can't think— The ladies," she finally managed in a gasp.

"See, Holly, I told you they're up here. Those are Nora's sneakers and Jake's legs and— Oh!"

"Molly, dear, we may have picked a most inopportune time. Let's leave before they see us."

"Well, at least they're getting along better!"

Nora buried her head in Jake's shoulder as they listened to the two sexagenarians retreat. Jake's chest shook. He was laughing, she realized. She lifted her head, then let out a whoop and began to laugh, as well.

"Nora, let's follow the excellent advice of our friends and leave. I want to make love to you in a bed."

She got up and buttoned her blouse. "Your bed or mine?"

"Yours. It's bigger."

"How do you know? Oh, never mind. I should know better than to ask a spook how he knows things he shouldn't."

"I'm a federal agent," he corrected patiently.

"Whatever."

Back at the hotel lobby, Nora stopped. "Give me a few minutes before you come. I want to freshen up and—" she smiled wickedly "—slip into something more comfortable."

"Ten minutes."

FIFTEEN MINUTES LATER—he wanted Nora to be as anxious for him as he was for her—Jake knocked on Nora's door. Although he'd spent the time wondering what he was getting himself into, he was unwilling to turn back. He was behaving like a fool but he might as well die with a smile on.

No one answered as he opened the door. The curtains were drawn, the room dark. "Nora?" Stepping inside, he saw her waiting for him in the bed.

He smiled, pulled back the sheets and froze. A knife was sticking out of the pillows arranged like a body. A lace confection was draped over the form, a stain where the knife had pierced it. Jake touched the warm liquid.

It was blood.

14

Rest and relaxation, that's what Merry Travelers is famous for. Yes, the sights and sounds can be a dizzying blur, but we always ensure there are days of leisure. You can enjoy fine dining, slow walks and general lazing about. Your friends will comment on how fresh and relaxed you look!

JAKE TORE OPEN the curtains, letting in the light. He saw the signs of the struggle he'd missed in the dark room: a bottle of overturned perfume, its sweet odor making the room claustrophobic, and a broken vase. Throwing open a window he turned back to the bed. A piece of paper fluttered on a playful breeze. Picking it up, he read, "Get off the case if you want to see her alive again."

Lucci's men had finally found his weak spot. They were gambling he cared enough about Nora to abandon the case. The case wasn't worth more to him than Nora, but he knew that even if he did what they wanted, Nora wouldn't be freed. What Lucci's men wanted was time to finish up this operation and hide all its traces. They'd simply run it again in a few months when the heat had died down.

He wouldn't let them get away with this. And his theory about never becoming involved was proved correct once again. Only this time it wasn't him who was in danger. If he didn't care about Nora they wouldn't have threatened her.

He'd get her back. And then he'd make sure she was never in danger again.

He ran to the lobby and caught Molly and Holly as they entered. He needed help, and he was going to trust his instincts about who cared for Nora and wanted her returned safely.

Molly looked surprised to see him. "Jake, you're here! Why, we weren't expecting to see you back so soon."

"Ladies, I need your help." He led them to a cluster of chairs and waited as they settled themselves expectantly. He would take advantage of resources Lucci's men wouldn't be expecting. "I'm an agent with the U.S. Customs department," he began slowly, not wanting to shock the pair.

"We were right." Molly practically bounced in her seat.

"Damn, did everyone know I wasn't a regular bus driver?" At Molly's raised eyebrow, he continued, "Never mind, I was just thinking out loud. I need your help with my investigation." Quickly he outlined the case, leaving out Nora's disappearance.

"We thought it was diamonds—that someone was smuggling diamonds." At Jake's puzzled look, Holly continued, "We were curious, that's why we were following you."

"It's not a game anymore." As much as he didn't want to scare the two friends, he had to show them how serious the situation was. "They've taken Nora."

"What do you mean?"

"They've kidnapped her. If I don't stop the investigation, they've threatened to kill her."

All of their bright enthusiasm was gone. "This is dreadful. Shouldn't you, we, do what they want?" Molly asked.

"No." He knew they wouldn't want to believe him but it was what experience had taught him. Their scared faces reflected his own concern. "If I do what they want, they'll still . . . hurt Nora. I know these men. If what they're involved in is worth this risk, they won't leave any loose ends. I need you to find Nora."

"But how can we?"

"Gaspé isn't a very large town, and I've seen how well you talk to strangers—" Like Nora. "I need your eyes and ears."

"We'll get the others to help us."

"No. Some of the group are involved. We can't let them know what we're up to." Jake stood and paced. The ladies were right; if they had more manpower they could cover a lot more ground faster. "Right," he said. "Tim and John Chance can help us."

"And Zachary," Holly added.

"No. I haven't cleared him."

"Don't be foolish," Molly said. "Oh, at first we suspected him, too, but then we figured out what he was doing. He'd want to help Nora." At Jake's scowl, she added, "Don't you know? He's the backer for her tour company. Zachary was one of Nora's professors and her thesis adviser. He was always fond of her and they kept in touch after Nora left university. When Zachary won the lottery he decided to invest in a business— Nora's business."

"*He* won the lottery?"

"Yes. He wanted to leave the classroom and try the real world. He's been on countless bus tours this past year, gathering information. Why, we've run into him several times."

As Nora said, there were lots of simple explanations. "I'll get Zachary, you get the Chance brothers and meet me in my room."

The war party gathered a long fifteen minutes later.

"This is outrageous!" Zachary bellowed. "You, young man," he pointed at Jake "—I hold you responsible. Imagine a U.S. agent helping Nora get kidnapped."

Jake restrained his anger. "I didn't help—"

"Never mind that now." Zachary waved off Jake's words. "I have the plans of the town." He pulled out a sheaf of papers from his attaché case. "Here, we can land the helicopters and SWAT teams here and here—" he moved his stubby finger over the map "—and then search the town."

"There's no backup," Jake said coldly.

"What! It's just us?" Zachary demanded.

"Yes. If the kidnappers see any firepower moving in they'll . . . hurt Nora."

"Oh." Zachary looked crushed. "But we must save Nora!"

"We will," Jake assured him and outlined his plan. Nora was being held somewhere nearby and he needed to know where. It should be simple for them to find out about strangers in town. With only one hotel, any strangers who weren't tourists would stand out. Jake was counting on it.

His small group was scared but determined. Their concern for Nora showed on their faces. "Remember, trust no one else. We don't know who is involved." Everyone nodded.

Holly rose to her feet like a head cheerleader. "We'll find her, Jake. You can count on us."

Jake hoped she was right. He had another lead to follow.

THE WARM AFTERNOON was giving way to the first hints of a cool evening when Jake found Bruce. The owner of Merry Travelers was all over a long-legged brunette on one of the secluded benches.

Jake's angry glower caught the attention of the woman first. She removed Bruce's head from her chest.

"Can't you see that I'm busy?" Bruce snapped.

Jake pulled Bruce to his feet and hit him hard. It felt so good that he was tempted to haul Bruce up from the grass and hit him again.

The girl—Jake recognized her from the concierge's desk—stared at Jake with awe. She rearranged her blouse to show more of the area Bruce had been exploring. "*Mon Dieu, monsieur.* You are very strong. But why did you hit him? Has he been fooling around with your woman?"

"Yes."

She marched over the still prone Bruce. "*Cochon!*" She kicked him hard.

After the brunette had stormed off, Jake waited for Bruce to turn a living color. When he'd stopped gasping like a dry-docked fish, Jake grabbed Bruce by the collar and hauled him up. On shaky feet, with Jake still exerting a death grip, Bruce croaked, "What the hell...? You're fired!" He broke Jake's hold and took an unsteady step backward. "I'm going to make sure no one ever hires you."

"Be quiet."

"You can't tell me what to do." When Jake stepped forward, Bruce backed up but continued, "You caught me unawares. That's why you managed to sucker punch me. You'd never have touched me otherwise." Bruce's retreat was stopped by a tree.

Jake grabbed him by the throat. "You can't fire me because I don't work for you...and I'd enjoy nothing more than tearing you apart but I need information. Nora's been taken. Where is she?"

"What?" Jake tightened his hands around Bruce's throat, then eased a little. "No one is supposed to get hurt." Beads of sweat broke out on Bruce's forehead.

"Where is she?"

"I don't know." At Jake's furious look, Bruce begged, "Honestly, I don't want Nora hurt."

"Where are you meeting Lucci's men?"

"I'm not." The pressure tightened. "They were supposed to get rid of you," Bruce gasped. "Please. I didn't know any of the details ... I swear.... I didn't want to get involved."

"How many are there?"

"Two, maybe three. Honest, I don't know anything else. I never wanted them to hurt Nora. She's special to me."

"How special?" Jake's words were frighteningly calm.

"She's an attractive woman ... and I've always had a weakness for her," Bruce choked out.

"You're lying. Nora would never have anything to do with you.... How long has Lucci been using your buses?" When Bruce began to turn a disconcerting purple, Jake released him and pulled out his badge. "I'm a U.S. Customs agent, and you're under arrest for—"

"Jake! We've found her!"

Molly's voice broke through his cloud of rage and Jake turned. Molly and Holly, along with Zachary, stood there. Both ladies opened and closed their mouths several times at the cold anger glittering on his face before any words squeaked out.

"Oh, my goodness gracious!" Molly looked as if she'd like to collapse along with Bruce.

"Lord, love a duck! I'd never have imagined ..." Resolutely Holly pushed her glasses back up her nose.

"Leave poor Bruce alone. He's got enough to worry about without you accosting him."

"He's up to his eyeballs in this."

"Why, you dirty rotten scoundrel!" Holly quickly turned her defense of Bruce into offense. "I always said you were no good." She raised her purse high, hitting Bruce first on the head, and when he raised his arms to protect himself, smacking him in the gut.

"Oof, no, I swear, Mrs. Wentworth, I never knew anyone would be hurt." Bruce flailed his arms about ineffectively as the deadly handbag continued its assault—first on his head, then his knees, his shoulder, his knees again. Bruce finally caught Holly's wrists, but he only held her away from him. "I'm truly sorry, Mrs. Wentworth. I never wanted anything bad to happen."

Reluctantly admiring Bruce for taking the blows rather than hurting the elderly woman, Jake pointed to the Chance brothers who had just caught up. "You two keep watch over Davis. I don't want him warning anyone. Now, ladies and Mr. Buch, you can show me where you found Nora."

IT HADN'T TAKEN MUCH questioning by the ever-inquisitive duo to learn which houses had been rented for the summer by outsiders. Dividing up the short list, they had quickly ascertained via the tricycles and other children's paraphernalia, that all the houses except one were rented by families.

Their destination lay on a lane as quiet as the rest of the town. Unlike the other houses, though, no laundry hung on the lines, and the shades were drawn.

"Should we not contact the local authorities?" Zachary asked as he crouched behind a lilac bush.

"And say what? We don't have any proof."

"But your position, Mr. Collins. Surely they would listen to an agent of the U.S. government." Mr. Buch's faith in the established order was being sorely tested.

"Yes, you're right, but that would take too long and give our men time to escape. No, I'll get up to the house and see if I can find where they're keeping Nora."

The windows at the front of the house were all drawn and locked tight. He could pick one of the locks easily enough, but first he had to find Nora. A look back revealed that his three compatriots were out of sight, although a flash of Molly's fuchsia hat indicated their anxious surveillance of his activities.

Keeping low and next to the house, he made his way to the back. An old swing tied to a big oak remembered better days. He hoped Nora wasn't too frightened; she had to know he'd save her. If anyone had hurt her he would make them wish they'd chosen bomb defusion as a safer career.

The back of the house had two windows, both with their shades up as the only view was of the thick forest beyond. The first room was a parlor and from the tangle of sheets thrown on the old-fashioned sofa, the sleeping place of someone. In the next room, the kitchen, he found Nora dealing out a hand of cards to her three abductors.

How could she! Here he was, worried sick about her, and she was going on as if she were organizing another tour. When he got her out of this he'd— The illogic of his argument broke in but Jake didn't care. It was time Nora behaved more like a regular person than the constantly cheerful, ever-efficient organizer with the oversize purse.

Again he carefully studied the scene before him. Nora was sitting to the side of the window and she couldn't see him unless he drew her attention and, as a consequence, that of the others. As he expected, her famous tote bag was by her chair—she'd probably pulled the deck of cards from it. He committed the kitchen layout to memory, including the guns strapped to each man.

After he'd returned to his gang and outlined his plan, Molly grumbled from the other side of the lilac bush, "Are you sure it wouldn't be better if Holly and I knocked on the front door? After all, who'd suspect two harmless little old ladies?"

"The last thing I'd ever call you is harmless. These men have been following us for days and they'll remember you two. Zachary, however, is less memorable and a master of deception." At Zachary's uncomfortable look, Jake smiled. "He's going to make a sweet little old lady...."

Moments later, Jake handed him the dress Molly had removed. "With this kerchief and makeup, they won't have any idea who you are."

When Holly had finished working her artistry, Zachary Buch was indeed unrecognizable. The dress was too tight, but he left the back zipper undone and threw Holly's raincoat over to cover it. The result was a very attractive woman.

"You'll do. Maybe you'll even get a date," Jake said.

"I don't know about those hairy legs," Holly warned.

"Just pretend he's European. You can speak German, can't you, Mr. Buch?"

"Certainly. I was reading the original works of Goethe before you were born, Mr. Collins," sniffed Zachary.

"Let's go, then."

As Zachary began to slowly mince his way up the gravel path in high heels, Holly and Molly followed Jake to the back. "Molly," her friend whispered, "Jake made *two* jokes."

Molly was picking a very careful path in her bare feet and tugging on Zachary's shirt to cover more of herself. "I told you Nora would be good for him. Now, if only he'd realize it!"

BACK AT HIS DESIGNATED spot by the kitchen window, Jake waited. A knock at the front door unnerved the three men, and each pulled out his gun. The leader, a strapping blond-haired muscleman, gestured to the small dark-haired man. He put his gun back in his holster, shrugged on his jacket and went down the hallway. The third goon, a short but pumped-up guy with a buzz cut, remained undisturbed. Nora shuffled the cards again, a serene smile on her face. Jake couldn't hear the door opening but he did hear Zachary Buch's falsetto demand, *"Wie ist Frau Binderschmidt? Ich bin..."*

The man's confused response was drowned out by Zachary's increasingly shrill diatribe.

"Damn." The blond goon stood, pointing his gun at Nora.

She met his gaze and said, "The woman is lost. She was supposed to visit her friend who is renting a house but this is the third place she's been to and no one has heard of her friend, or speaks a word of German."

"And how do you?"

"I'm a tour guide, remember? It's part of my job."

The sound of breaking glass in the room next door froze the two remaining men. "Damn. Something's going on. You," the blonde said to his companion, "go see—and don't be afraid to shoot."

Jake prayed that Holly and Molly would follow his plan exactly and prepared to make his move. The blonde's killer eyes stared at Nora with distrust. "I knew you were trouble. I should have done you in like the other one." He pressed his gun to Nora's temple and cocked the trigger.

Jake heard the argument in the hall turn into the unmistakable sounds of a fight. Another window broke and Holly shouted, "Now! Now!"

"If someone tries for you, kaboom, your brains will be splattered all over that wall." The killer pointed to his head and Jake hurled himself through the window, promising anything if he could keep the ugly son of a bitch from pulling the trigger.

A scream of rage was instantly followed by a shot. Sick, Jake rolled clear of the shattered glass and jumped to his feet, gun raised, ready to kill.

At his feet lay the blonde, rubbing at his eyes, screaming, "You bitch. I'm gonna get you for this!"

Nora was standing on shaky feet, a quivery smile on her face.

"How? What?" Jake picked up the gun.

"I maced him." Nora revealed the can of mace she held in her hand. Then her eyes filled with tears and she threw herself at Jake. He wrapped his arms tightly around her and buried his face in her hair. At Holly's shout of triumph he relaxed—his intrepid senior citizens had subdued the two gunmen.

"It's okay, baby. It's all okay. I won't let anyone hurt you."

Nora raised her gaze to his, but his eyes seemed to be out of focus because of moisture. "I knew you'd rescue me. Every girl needs her own spy, secret agent—hero," she said with her familiar sarcasm. And then she kissed him.

15

Merry Travelers tours offer lots of opportunities
for you to learn about the world around you!

"IT'S A money-laundering operation."

"What?"

"I don't understand."

They were back in Jake's room once again, but with
Nora this time, nursing various bruises and celebrating victory. Nora sat next to Jake on the bed, his arm
wrapped possessively around her shoulders.

Nora hadn't really been frightened until after it was
over. She studied her intrepid rescuers with fondness.
Holly and Molly looked as if they were ready to explode with everything that had happened. The tele-
phone company would soon be making a handsome
profit from the pair's retelling of events. And, for once,
there would be no need for any embellishment—what
they had accomplished was Olympian. Nora would
never forget Molly and Holly charging into the kitchen
brandishing a flat, thick piece of wood—a swing seat,
she'd later discovered—after the gunshot. They had
used it to break windows, distracting the dark-haired
thug. They had disobeyed Jake's orders and knocked
him out with it when he'd investigated the noise.

"Nora, you're all right!" Molly had declared, fully prepared to take on any leftover bad guys.

"Oh, thank you, thank you!" Holly had added and the two had thrown themselves at Nora and Jake.

When Zachary Buch arrived moments later, with kerchief askew, several buttons missing and arms wide, Jake had quickly stepped aside, leaving the women for Zachary's bearlike hug.

That's when the reality of the situation had hit: Jake cuffing the man on the floor; Holly and Molly proudly unveiling the suspect they had knocked unconscious; and Zachary retrieving the man he'd trussed up in the hallway with the belt from Holly's coat. Nora had been surrounded by her friends, but Jake had hung back, away from the circle of intimacy. After that one emotional outburst, it was if he had already left her life. Even now, while he was holding her, she sensed that he had already gone.

She'd lost him before she'd ever really had a chance. Sure, half the time neither had trusted the other—but still there'd been something between them, something she'd never experienced with any other man. And Jake needed to learn to listen to her advice. But now that there was nothing keeping them apart it seemed as if Jake was determined that nothing would keep them together. Well, she wasn't one to give up so easily....

There was a quick rap at the door, and Holly opened it to reveal a tall, good-looking woman. The last of Nora's few hopes died.

"E.J.!" Jake said. "What the devil are you doing here? The doctors—"

"Would like to keep me in the hospital forever. But you know me better than that, Jake. I thought I'd be arriving to give you a helping hand, but from the reports I heard on the police radio it sounds like you've got the case all wrapped up." The woman's voice was melodious, confident.

"We have some of Lucci's henchmen but we haven't actually caught anyone doing anything illegal—except for Nora's kidnapping, of course." Jake crossed the room and kissed E.J. on the mouth as Nora seethed. "So I've saved the good part for you."

"You know what's going on?"

"Money laundering."

Jake faced all the curious expressions. "It took me a long time to figure it out, especially since so many of you led me such a merry chase, but after I crossed all of you off my list of suspects, the answer was obvious. Our Happy Days gang has spent most of its time popping in and out of banks."

At the group's continued silence, E.J. picked up the story. "Of course. With all these innocent-looking passengers and because we paid special attention to the buses coming back into the States, not going *into* Canada, they could transport a lot of money into Canada."

E.J. was also smart, Nora noted sourly.

At the continued silence, Jake shifted uncomfortably and cleared his throat. "I'd like you all to meet E.J.

Sullivan." Jake introduced the Merry Travelers to E.J., Nora last. While Nora had met the woman as Emma at the Merry Travelers office, Nora looked at her with new eyes. Not only was E.J. an undercover agent, but Jake liked her. A lot.

"Emma Jane," she said as she shook Nora's hand. "I prefer Emma Jane. Jake is the only one who can't seem to use it."

"But what are we going to do now?" Molly demanded. "I still don't understand."

"Are you sure it's not diamonds?" Holly added hopefully.

"No, ladies, I'm afraid the glamorous crimes are rarely ones we get to investigate." Jake smiled at the two disappointed women, and then began to pace, caught up in his thinking. He hadn't looked at her once, Nora realized despondently. Not since E.J. had arrived. "But money laundering is a big part of any criminal organization. Obviously Lucci had a very efficient operation going here. Canadian banks have looser laws than their American counterparts. It's easier to make deposits of ten thousand dollars—especially if you're a sweet white-haired grandmother with fake ID. One or two individuals could visit five or six banks in a day, maybe more. On a week-long tour, half a million to a million dollars could easily be cleared—and after each deposit the money begins a series of untraceable electronic transfers until it ends up in one of Lucci's holding companies."

"Brilliant," said Emma Jane. "That's why I wasn't able to trace a pattern when it came to destinations. All the buses needed to do was cross the border and stay in Canada for several banking days. That was the connection I'd uncovered. Nice work, Jake, as usual." She smiled warmly at everyone. "But it looks like you had a good team."

"I did, but all we have right now is a theory. Lucci's men aren't talking and neither is Bruce Davis. Luckily the paperwork on the arrests has been misplaced so Lucci doesn't know we've broken part of the ring."

"So we can set a trap," announced Zachary Buch, warming up to the theories. "We will catch the culprits in action."

"Alicia Hall and Ben Riley," said Nora.

"Yes." Jake finally looked at her, his eyes warm. Nora melted. "They've been in and out of banks throughout the trip. At first I didn't think anything of it, but the number of visits began to make me very curious."

"Plus they're two-timing Harold and Janet," Holly chimed in.

"Exactly." Her words earned a rueful grin from Jake. "Do you two know everything that's going on?"

"Just about," Holly said with satisfaction.

"But why," asked John Chance, "didn't those involved simply cross over into Canada in a car and stay for as long as they wanted?"

"Because of the anonymity of bus travel. Customs doesn't keep lists of passengers but we'd notice if certain individuals were constantly crossing the border. I also wouldn't be surprised if some of the seniors were duped into making deposits, never realizing what they were doing was illegal.

"We still need to set up a trap. Anyone have any ideas?" E.J. asked.

"Yes." With Molly and Holly, Zachary Buch and the Chance brothers offering advice, Jake and E.J. planned. Once Jake looked up and asked Nora what she thought of something that had been suggested, but she hadn't been listening to a word, so she merely nodded and smiled.

She had her own plans to make.

"THIS IS GOING TO BE MORE exciting than my second honeymoon!" exclaimed Molly.

"What about your first?" asked Holly.

"A complete disappointment."

"It's not as dangerous as when we rescued Nora."

"That's why it's more exciting! Then, I was too scared and nervous," Molly said. "That was the meat and potatoes of the meal, this is the dessert.

"Look, there she goes!" Holly and Molly were following Alicia, who had just entered a bank. Supremely confident, they sidled close to their target, able to hear her begin a conversation in excellent French.

"I never knew she could speak French!" Holly whispered.

"She's not likely to have told us she's capable of conducting illegal transactions in a foreign tongue. Now hush up and listen!"

"That's it, she just said her name was Madame Hertha Martine."

Molly removed her hat and fanned herself as their prearranged signal to Emma Jane who'd been busy pretending to find a pen that worked to fill out a deposit slip. She moved quickly, showing her badge to a startled teller and restraining Alicia Hall.

"This is an outrage," Alicia cried. "Since when is it illegal to make a deposit?"

"When the money is from a crime syndicate and you use false identification."

"Nonsense. This is my money and the teller must have misunderstood my French."

"These ladies—" Emma Jane pointed to Holly and Molly "—overheard every word of your conversation and will swear out a statement to that fact. And—" Emma Jane reached for Alicia's purse, extracting her wallet and pulling out a dozen pieces of identification "—you might want to tell me why you travel with so many aliases."

Holly and Molly watched as Emma Jane marched Alicia out the door to the police station, where E.J. would begin the paperwork for Alicia's extradition to the States. "That was smooth. She's very good!"

"I'm sure Jake took down—" Holly giggled "—Ben Riley just as well."

"Once again all I can say, my dear friend, is thank you for insisting we take this tour. I never imagined bus travel could be so much fun!"

AFTER THE CELEBRATORY dinner, which Emma Jane missed because she wanted to finish the paperwork on the arrests, Jake was back in his hotel room. He'd agreed to drive the bus to the border tomorrow, where Nora had made arrangements for a replacement driver to take over. Tonight was the first time since starting the trip that he'd be able to spend the night in his room instead of skulking around the hallways.

He opened the door and went down the corridor, aimlessly, until he was in front of Nora's door. He should thank her for her help and say goodbye. She'd been preoccupied throughout dinner and he wanted to . . . explain.

Hell, he wanted to make love with her again, but he knew that was a terrible idea. Being with Nora wasn't simple. Every time he looked at her, touched her, made saying goodbye that much harder. Emotional involvement was not what he wanted.

Nora did. He'd known that from the beginning. He'd also seen it in her eyes ever since he'd rescued her. She was caught up in the adventure, was picturing him as a hero. What she'd forgotten was that he was also the reason she'd been in danger.

And if he'd really loved her, he wouldn't have been so willing to believe that she might be the guilty party. Nora couldn't build any kind of life with a man who always suspected the worst.

No, the best thing for both of them would be if he left now.

He knocked on her door.

Nora opened it, looking slightly flustered. "Oh, good, now I won't have to look for you. Come in."

He followed her in. She'd been coming to look for him dressed like that? The white satin nightgown hugged her curves and was held up by straps that threatened to fall and leave her soft breasts bared to his ravenous gaze. The sheer robe that she wore unbelted, teased more than it covered. "You were coming to look for me?" His voice sounded harsh to his own ears.

"I wanted a chance to say goodbye in private."

Her quiet words made him angry. Nora deserved a lot better than him. "You'd better put some clothes on. I can't think when you're dressed like that."

"That's your problem, Special Agent Collins. You think too much. What do you feel when I touch you like this?" Nora brushed her lips against his, then pressed small kisses along his jaw. He held himself immobile against her attack, but the pulse under his ear belied his calm.

"Stop that." Despite the fact that he wanted to hold her, to bury himself inside her and promise her everything, he held himself completely still. If Nora was overcome by the situation, he, at least, would keep a sane head; would rescue her from himself.

When she used her lips to explore that erratic pulse, he gripped her shoulders and held her away from him. "Stop that. I don't want you."

"You're lying." Nora's voice shook. She was afraid. All the feeling couldn't be one-sided, could it?

Jake dropped his arms and moved away from her. "I don't want to want you."

Relief washed over her. "Why not?"

"It can get you hurt. Look what happened today. Lucci's men knew we were...involved. That's why they kidnapped you. If it hadn't been for me, you would never have been in any danger."

"You also saved me."

The silence stretched and grew taut as neither was willing to concede the other's point.

"I also suspected you, Nora."

"I know."

"We're too different, you believe everything good and I look for what is bad."

"We made a good team. I'm not always right, Jake. There was an illegal operation going on with my passengers and my boss. I won't be quite as trusting next time."

"In my work, you learn not to trust anyone—not even your partner."

"You trust Emma Jane," Nora persisted.

"E.J. is good, but I only partner with her occasionally. I was burned badly once. I'm not willing to take that risk again. I work better alone."

"And you call her E.J. so you won't have to think about her as a woman. There are other agents who must trust their partners. And agents who are married with families," She was becoming desperate.

"I work better alone," he insisted doggedly.

"You're afraid," she taunted.

"Don't be ridiculous."

"You're afraid of me because you can't forget I'm a woman and you want me."

"Damn you," he said quietly, and then she was in his arms and he was kissing her. When she'd forgotten how to breathe, forgotten what planet she was on, he let go of her.

After gulping in air, and picking up her robe, which had somehow ended up on the floor, Nora dared to look at Jake. He was shirtless and sitting on her bed, pulling off his boots.

"What are you doing?"

"I'm undressing so you can have an easier time of seducing me. That is what you were planning on in that gown, weren't you?" He stripped, revealing his magnificent body, and pulled down the sheets, then lay down on the bed, nonchalantly crossing his arms behind his head. "What are you waiting for? Weren't you going to prove to me how right we are together?" When Nora didn't move, he patted the bed. "Come on over here, honey, I'm ready."

Was he ever! she thought, as she approached the bed warily. This wasn't at all how she'd played out the scenario in her mind. He was trying to reduce what they had to sex.

She knew it was a lot more than that. Why, the entire time she'd been held hostage, all she'd been able to think about was the mistakes she'd made with Jake. She should have believed him instead of insisting on doing everything her way.

Jake was just as bad.

If they had any kind of future together they'd fight all the time. He'd want things his way, she'd disagree. She'd find the positive side, he'd see the negative. It would be great.

But how could she convince him?

Nora stepped toward him, determined to try. "You can't frighten me off so easily."

"Who wants to scare you away?" His gaze raked her body and he smiled. He wanted to convince her all they had was sex so he cupped her breasts, his thumbs rubbing the satiny material against her aroused flesh.

"You don't play fair," she gasped. Her face was flushed and pretty; he didn't want to let her go, ever.

He pulled her down on top of him, needing to feel all of her. He didn't care why he wanted Nora anymore. He simply did—more than he'd ever wanted any other woman. He kissed her gently and then harder. Branding her lower lip with his teeth, he then lathed it with his tongue until Nora moaned. Rolling her onto her back, he took control as he rained kisses down her slender neck, caressing her breasts with his mouth and hands and then exploring the rest of her. She writhed beneath him, enjoying the onslaught. When he was poised over her, seeking entrance, he held himself in check, wanting to see Nora open her eyes. She did, and he saw passion, need and something else—something he didn't want to identify. He kissed her once quickly as he pressed himself into her and whispered, "It's more important that I play very well."

16

The ending of one of a Merry Traveler tour is never sad because of all the new friends you've made!

NORA DIDN'T NEED to entertain her passengers on the final day of this tour. From the hubbub, the group could have been celebrating the Super Bowl. She gazed fondly at them as they regaled each other with his or her part in the mystery and the capture of the criminals. Alicia Hall's and Ben Riley's arrests had been a shock to their companions. But now that Janet had gotten over being duped—that Ben had never been romantically interested in her, but had used her as a cover—she was joining in on the analysis. Harold Anderson, however, was sitting alone at the back of the bus. Nora feared it would take him some time to recover from the events.

Molly had even returned to cordial terms with Stephan Papas. The intrepid Wentworth-and-Terts duo had discovered that he'd been seeing another woman in Montreal—a much younger woman. Molly had confronted him about the little gold digger—those being the nicest words Molly had used. Stephan had sworn the young lady was a friend of his daughter's, in whom he had only a fatherly interest.

Molly was accepting the explanation, but Stephan was aware he was on shaky ground.

"It looks like your tourists had the trip of their lives." Emma Jane slid into the seat next to Nora. Nora saw Jake stare at them through the rearview mirror but no matter how hard he strained, he wouldn't be able to overhear them.

"They have reason to be happy," Nora agreed. The two women sat comfortably for a few minutes, Nora waiting for Emma Jane to say her piece.

"You and Jake made a good team."

"But Lucci is still free."

"We do what we can. This time we've crippled one of his operations. Next time we might get him."

"Is that what you go on for? The next time?"

"For now. It's not everything, Nora, but it'll do. But Jake thinks it's enough." Emma Jane stopped and took a deep breath. "Don't let his stubbornness stop you."

Nora understood what Emma Jane was trying to say. That she thought Jake might have some feeling for Nora, but he didn't want to admit to them. Well, she knew he had some...affection for her, but was it strong enough to break down the barriers Jake had erected? "He has to want a future...with me," Nora said quietly.

"Jake is purposely blind to some things, especially his emotions. And despite his decisiveness in his work he's very cautious about his personal life. For some reason he seems to think he's better off alone. He'll need time."

"I was worried he might be in love with you," Nora confessed.

"No, he feels far too comfortable with me. That's the last thing he feels with you. You're in love with him, aren't you?"

"Yes."

Emma Jane patted her hand. They didn't speak anymore about Jake for the rest of the trip. Too soon for Nora's liking, they were at the border. Numbly, she watched the customs officer speed the bus through procedures and the new driver approach.

Jake walked down the aisle of the bus saying farewell to his happy campers. It seemed so easy for him to leave. Nora wondered sourly how many broken hearts Jake Collins had left behind.

"Ladies, I expect a postcard from your next excursion. Try not to cause too much trouble." He smiled his killer smile at them and Nora frowned.

"Why, never!" Holly and Molly exclaimed in unison.

"But you've whetted our appetite for adventure. We're going to take one of those delightful mystery cruises."

"Alone?" Jake teased.

"Those charming Chance brothers will be joining us."

"And Stephan Papas," Molly added.

"Molly, that's going to be a bit awkward. Three of them, two of us."

Jake left the two in heated debate. Only Nora was left. He'd spent hours rationalizing his decision and practicing the right words, but now that he was in front of her, he couldn't remember them. He wasn't even sure if he was really making the right decision. "Nora, I . . ."

She lifted her face and he saw that her eyes were filled with tears. "Damn. I never wanted to hurt you."

It was hurting him, but he told himself for the hundredth time this morning, that it was for the best. It wasn't possible to fall in love in only a week. He didn't want to settle down; he valued his freedom. Love only led to complications. Soon he'd be resenting her and how she'd tied him down. A mortgage and diapers! He wanted good memories of Nora, not bitterness.

Even ignoring the fact that he and Nora would drive each other crazy trying to control the relationship, he didn't want a future with any woman—and certainly not a controlling, overbearing one like Nora.

Then again, the women he usually dated didn't captivate his attention like Nora did. Didn't have him actually contemplating the white-picket-fence dream. No, it would definitely be a mistake.

He'd be saving himself a lot of hurt in the future. Nora might call him a coward—and he wouldn't completely deny the accusation—but it was smarter this way.

They'd only known each other for a week.

He'd forget her soon.

Her attempt at a smile was pathetic. "I know you didn't promise me anything. In fact you warned me. I'll be all right. And, I have a business to start. It's what I've dreamed about, planned for years, so I don't really have time for anything else in my life right now. You'd better go."

Jake looked at her, wanting to say something, but he didn't have anything to say. He wanted to leave. He didn't want involvement, he didn't want to say anything about love and forever. He didn't believe in that. No, he was definitely better off alone.

Jake turned away from Nora and walked through the bus for the last time, aware that every pair of eyes was on his retreating back. He saw Molly and Holly shake their heads as he passed.

At the steps he stopped and almost turned around. Instead, he left.

NORA PUT DOWN THE PHONE and yelled for her new partner. "We got it! The Japanese are signing with us!"

Maureen Davis ran in. "Wonderful news, but I knew you'd convince them. You're the best salesperson I've ever met." She peered at the papers in her hand. "With this deal, plus the group you signed up last week, the figures look good. Soon Merry Travelers will be out of the red."

"If everything works out like we hope. There's still a lot of potholes ahead." Despite her cautionary words, Nora couldn't contain her glee. Ever since Mrs. Davis had sold her fifty-one percent of Merry Travelers, business had been getting better. And Zach had suggested that he had a lead on another investor for their company. With some more capital, she could make Merry Travelers extremely profitable.

At first she'd been flabbergasted by Maureen Davis's offer, especially since Bruce was currently serving his term behind bars. But Mrs. Davis—Maureen—had been adamant. She hadn't given the company to her son because she hadn't been able to let go. "Which," as she'd explained to Nora at that surprising meeting five months ago, "was probably one of the reasons why Bruce did what he did. Don't get me wrong. I'm not excusing my son, but I do accept that what I did was wrong. If I'd really given him the company like I'd promised, he wouldn't have needed to prove to me how successful he could be. Unfortunately he's a terrible businessman—just like his father, which is also why I didn't want to give him control of the business—and he turned to an easier method of making money.

"I don't want to repeat my mistake. That's why I want to offer fifty-one percent to you."

"But why me? I don't understand."

"You've always impressed me, Nora, and I know you're ambitious. I know all about your plans to open your own company." At Nora's surprised look, she nodded. "I still have my sources. If you buy me out, you have majority control and the advantage of an established company."

"That's very generous of you—"

"Not all that generous. I want to come back. Retirement didn't agree with me, but I don't have the energy for fifteen-hour days."

Maureen worked three days a week, which left her time for her hobbies and a visit to the beauty shop, she declared. In her early sixties, Maureen was sprightly and beautiful. Nora was surprised that she had never remarried. Maureen had explained that was because she had spent too much effort on her business and none on her social life—Nora had flinched guiltily under Maureen's telling look, but Maureen never lectured, only led by example—but that had all changed. And then she had winked at Zachary Buch. Zachary and Maureen always seemed to put in the same days at the office.

Nora spent all of her time there: planning new trips, making up budgets, listening to her employees' suggestions about how to make the trips better, selling—anything and everything that came across her desk. And she loved it. Or so she told herself.

After a celebratory clink of coffee cups, Maureen packed up to go home. "Don't stay too late."

"I'm only going to go through some mail and then I'm off, too." Nora idly flipped through the correspondence, separating the invoices from hotel brochures, stopping when she found a postcard.

The front pictured a full-color Sphinx. On the back, scrawled handwriting declared: "The Egyptian men are divine, but I just adore the mummies! Imagine, some of the kings had their servants and wives entombed with them—while still alive! Would have boded poorly for me in those times—my psychic has confirmed that I was Egyptian royalty. Love, Molly. P.S. Holly sends

you her love. P.P.S. Has he shown up *Yet?* The last word
was underlined several times.

No, he hadn't. Nora wondered if she'd ever really
expected him to.

But she had. She'd foolishly believed Jake was in love
with her and as soon as he realized it, he'd come after
her.

But Jake had told her he wouldn't. He had said
goodbye and he'd meant it. After five months, she had
to accept that reality.

A future for her and Jake was definitely one plan that
wasn't going to work out.

Nora pinned the postcard on her bulletin board next
to the dozen other the globe-trotting pair had sent. Each
card had asked hopefully about Jake.

She recalled her mantra of *Just three more trips,*
when the desire to start her own business had been
overwhelming. When she'd been convinced that being
an independent, successful career woman would make
her happy, she'd been wrong.

Making Merry Travelers competitive and profitable
was good. But not as good as having Jake.

It was time for her to stop hoping. With a last look
around the office, she shut off the lights.

She had Merry Travelers. That was enough.

17

After experiencing your first Merry Traveler tour you won't be able to wait for your next vacation with us!

JAKE HUNCHED himself into the shadows of the alleyway and waited.

The sound of a footstep had him pulling out his revolver and signaling to the man closest to him. He didn't dare speak into his microphone for fear of being overheard. He could see Eddie Mukler, the man he'd been after for the past two months, meet a man dressed in a dark jacket and jeans. Jake smiled—the deal had to be going down tonight.

He waited as the negotiations dragged on, but finally the money exchanged hands. Mukler nodded to one of his operatives and the cocaine was shown and tested.

A garbage can crashed in the stillness. Everyone froze—a tableau lit by the poor light of a streetlamp, then broken by the bright flare of automatic gunfire.

Jake pulled out his gun and ran forward in pursuit of Mukler. He knew his men were moving in, trying to cut off the exits, but he didn't want to leave Mukler to anyone except himself. Mukler was grabbing the briefcase full of money. He saw Jake running toward him and raised his revolver. "Freeze!" Jake yelled. "Federal officers."

Mukler turned and ran, with Jake after him. Two of Jake's men converged at the back of the alley. Mukler stopped realizing he had no way out. He turned and fired.

Jake felt the bullet rip through his shoulder as he tackled Mukler. In the ensuing confusion of voices and running steps, he rolled around in the dirt with Mukler. He had Mukler pinned under him, his good arm pressed tight against Mukler's throat, when Mukler kneed Jake and ended up on top.

"Damn," Jake swore as Mukler banged his head against the pavement. Pain filled his eyes as he used his bad arm to block Mukler's next blow. His good arm forced his gun under Mukler's chin. "You're under arrest."

Mukler glared at him with hatred and Jake could see him considering whether he had any chance of killing Jake before Jake shot him. If Mukler believed he had a chance, he'd take it. Mukler's eyes shifted; Jake waited. He felt Mukler tense and he pressed tighter on the trigger, ready—

Mukler threw aside his gun.

An agent hauled Mukler to his feet and began reading him his Miranda rights.

Jake breathed a sigh of relief, cursed the pain in his side and passed out.

"SO HOW'S THE HERO doing today?"

Jake scowled at E.J.'s beaming face. "What the hell is that?" he demanded when he saw the large stuffed pink bear she deposited at the foot of his bed. The bear grinned stupidly at him.

"The department pitched in for a get-well present." E.J. adjusted the bow around the bear's neck. "Don't you like him?"

"I outgrew toys years ago."

"Oh, I don't know." E.J. looked first at Jake, then at the bear. "I thought you'd suit because of how well you both growl."

Jake refused to respond and E.J. continued to fuss with the bow until she was satisfied. Finally she turned back to Jake. "What do the doctors say?"

"They're a bunch of old women. I have to stay here for another couple of days—I hate to think what they'd do if I was really hurt."

"You were lucky," E.J. agreed. Jake's injury was painful but not life-threatening. The shot had gone cleanly through his shoulder. Not that that had improved his mood any, she reflected. Jake had been demanding to leave the hospital ever since he'd been admitted. "What do you plan to do with your vacation?"

Jake scowled even more and E.J. studied her shoe to hide her smile. He was furious about his forced holiday.

"I don't need any time off."

"Jake, all you've done for the last five months is work. You've broken the department record for overtime." E.J. gathered all her courage and forged ahead before he could interrupt. "When Mukler had that gun on you, God, Jake, I was so scared."

"I was, too."

"At that second, when you realized it might all be over, wasn't there anything you wished you'd done differently in your life?"

Jake scowled at E.J. He knew damn well what she was getting at. He hadn't known that E.J. was such a stupid romantic until she'd begun harassing him about Nora. He hardly remembered his little fling with Nora Stevens, he lied to himself. "Contrary to popular belief, my life did not flash before my eyes. I was just afraid Mukler was going to pull the trigger. I was lucky it was only a shoulder wound."

E.J. sighed. She couldn't force something out of Jake that he wasn't willing to admit. Instead, she filled him in on the recent exploits of their department. She made him laugh with the latest practical joke. She'd stayed too long already but as she kissed him goodbye, she couldn't resist one last try.

"The guys gave me the money, so I picked out the bear because it was such a silly present for you. It was funny." She was at the door but she turned and looked at him levelly. "Do you have any fun anymore?"

Jake had been wondering that all too often over the past few months. The investigations, the arrests, even the convictions didn't give him the same satisfaction they used to. Gone were the heady days when it had been a thrill. Something was missing.

And he knew damn well what it was.

Nora.

He remembered everything about her. How she walked. Her smell. Her silly organizational charts. How she'd made him smile. How brave she'd been when he left her. The soft sounds she'd made when they made love.

His longed-for freedom just didn't have the appeal it used to. What was the point of it when he couldn't share his good moments with someone?

Nora Steven had ruined him.

NORA LOOKED DOWN the street, quelling the urge to tap her foot. Damn, the driver was late.

She shoved a hand through her loose hair—no pink bows or pink anything for her anymore. One of the first changes she'd initiated at Merry Travelers was the abolition of the dreaded polyester uniforms. The guides had been effusive in their thanks, which made Francine's 5:00 a.m. call all the more unforgivable. Francine had interrupted what little sleep Nora managed these nights to announce that she was phoning from a Las Vegas wedding chapel where she'd just tied the knot and wouldn't be able to meet her tour group this morning. Even worse, she'd expected Nora to be happy for her. *Love!* It sucked.

At that time in the morning Nora hadn't been able to call any of her other escorts and had been forced instead to throw a few clothes into a bag and dig out her spare set of bingo cards before rushing to the pickup spot. She'd made it with seconds to spare for the 7:00 a.m. departure, but no bus, no driver. In fact—Nora scanned the front of the Omni Hotel, there was no group of milling tourists, either. Could Francine have told her the wrong pickup point?

Just then she spied the bus, making its awkward turn into the parking lot. The driver had to back up once to make the angle. Great. She had a new guy. Watching the bus pull alongside her, Nora wondered what she had done to deserve this while scatterbrained Francine was off on her honeymoon. She'd probably snagged a rich husband, as well—probably the only good-looking, rich single man under fifty-five ever to have taken a Merry Travelers—

The hairs on the back of her neck prickled as the door of the bus opened. She stepped on board to find Jake behind the wheel. She blinked once. He was still there, looking great in a pair of jeans and denim shirt. She pinched herself hard because she'd also dreamed this situation once. The pinch hurt.

"You're late," was the only thing she could think to say.

About five months too late, Jake agreed silently, finding it hard to look at her. Where was all of his bravery when he really needed it? He turned off the engine and then stood. "Hi," was all he could say.

Nora found the space between them much too small; she stepped down the aisle. His voice sounded even better than she remembered. She felt all flustered and out of control. And mad. What was Jake Collins doing here just as she was getting used to the idea that she was never going to see him again? She turned and glared at him.

"You're mad at me," he said calmly, as if seeing her again was easy. He met her gaze evenly and she wondered if this was how he operated at work, always so calm and aloof. When he dropped his eyes to survey her, her hand involuntarily brushed back her bangs. She knew she looked pale from too many hours trapped behind her desk. And too many nights losing sleep over him, although she'd never admit to that. She'd lost weight, as well.

"You look like hell," he said.

He looked wonderful.

"What are you doing here?" she asked coldly. Glancing out the window she still didn't see any would-be passengers and realized she'd been set up.

"I'm on vacation," Jake answered. "I thought we could take a trip together."

She couldn't believe the arrogance of the man. He knew damn well that he'd broken her heart when he left. Now, without one word for five months—almost half a year!—he was back. Wanting to take a vacation. A nice little no-strings-attached fling! She scowled and wondered if she could hit him hard enough to hurt him.

Under her furious stare, Jake shifted uncomfortably. "Nora—"

"That's it? You want me to go on a bus trip with you?" Nora demanded.

"Yes." Jake sighed. "Look, I know I was an idiot—"

"A pig."

"Okay, a pig."

"A . . . a skunk!"

Jake waited but Nora stopped and crossed her hands defensively across her chest. This was going to be as hard as he'd imagined. So much for his pleasant fantasy of Nora catching one glimpse of him and throwing herself into his arms.

"What would you like me to say?" he asked.

His words were in his usual even tones but his left hand was clenched tightly around an armrest, Nora noted.

"That you missed me desperately, that you love me and want to spend the rest of your life with me."

She didn't dare breathe as the tension stretched. She hadn't really meant to say that; the words had slipped out as a flip retort to cover her pain.

Then she hit him. Slugged him in the right shoulder.

To her complete surprise, Jake fell back, cradling his shoulder defensively. He turned toward her, his face pale.

"What's wrong with your shoulder?" Nora asked.

"Nothing."

"Tell me," she insisted. Her voice managed to remain calm despite her concern. Served him right. Let him think she didn't care.

Jake scowled at her. "It's a minor flesh wound."

"How long were you in the hospital?"

"A couple of days."

Nora felt sick. If she had a life with Jake, could she get used to this worry about him being hurt . . . killed?

"Is that why you're here?" she asked. "You almost died and realized there was something wrong with your life?" She hated to think that he'd come to her because he was scared. What about when the effects of his "divine revelation" diminished and he wanted his old life back? She didn't want him on the rebound from his work.

"It was nothing serious. My doctor was just overly cautious. All I did was get bored—I don't like being inactive." He pointedly studied her. "It looks like you've become more like me—all work and no play."

"Maybe that's not such a bad thing." Nora shrugged, "Running my own company is a lot of work, but it's worth it."

"Is it?"

"Yes." But she wanted so much more.

"Is that all you want?"

Nora suddenly found it hard to breathe normally. "What do you mean?"

"I missed you desperately." He walked toward her. "I love you." He stopped in front of her. "I want to spend the rest of my life with you."

He looked like he meant every word. Nora wanted him to, but she had to ask, "Are you sure?"

"I've never been surer of anything in my life." That's when she hit him on the left shoulder.

That shot didn't do anything except hurt Nora's hand. "How dare you," she exclaimed and whirled around, stomping down the aisle and back. "How dare you assume that you could just waltz back into my life and I'd be waiting for you! I'm over you, Jake Collins."

"You're not dating anyone else. I checked," Jake said flatly. "Wait—" he held up his hand in surrender "—don't hit me again. I know I'm an arrogant pigskunk to just walk back into your life and want you to love me, but I do."

"You think I love you?" she gasped, still angry, still disoriented. She didn't know if she believed his words. While she wondered what to do she realized that Jake had started the bus and they were pulling away from the hotel. He didn't pull onto the route for the expressway, but turned the vehicle foward a tree-shaded street. She grabbed a pole in remembrance of his crazy driving and demanded, "Where are we going?"

"I have you for a seven-day tour, and I plan to take full advantage of it. Especially as your new partner." Jake dared to take a quick look at her as he parked the bus on an isolated dead end and locked the door. He was afraid Nora might scream very loudly. He wondered if the windows were shatterproof.

"Zach pulled you in as our new partner?" Nora was disbelieving.

"I own fifteen percent. I hoped it would help you realize I was serious. Give me a chance, Nora, come with me."

"Where are we going?"

Jake's cheeks burned with pink as he replied, "Vegas."

"So that's where Francine got that crazy story from," Nora said, and then blinked. "Vegas . . . Jake, I'm not sure. . . ."

Jake touched her shoulders, running his hands along her arms and pulling her closer to him. She could feel his warm breath against her cheek, saw the fear in his eyes, and all her anger disappeared.

"Nora, I love you," Jake said and touched his lips to hers. It was like coming home, Nora thought. After that, she only felt . . . alive, happy, in love.

A long time later, Jake was sitting on a bus seat with Nora pressed tightly against him. Nora moved. "Am I hurting your wound?"

Jake pulled her closer. "I'm perfect like this."

Nora sighed with happiness. But she had to voice her doubts. "Jake, are you sure? Maybe your feelings for me are because of your injury. A brush with death can make you do all sorts of things you wouldn't normally, and wish you hadn't later on."

"For the last time, I was not mortally wounded. Besides, nothing in my life was any good since I left you."

Nora twisted to look at him. "Really?"

"You want every last confession out of me, don't you?"

"Yes."

"Okay. All the fun was gone. I wanted to tell you about my cases, make you laugh at my jokes, make love to you, make babies."

"Is that a proposal of marriage?"

"Woman, stop putting words into my mouth before I can get to them." He kissed her so thoroughly and completely that Nora lay her bemused head against his shoulder. "And yes, that was a proposal."

"But what are you going to do? You're not really quitting the force?"

"I can't, it's part of me. You understand that, don't you?"

Nora nodded. It would be tough but she'd get used to it. And it was better than not having Jake at all. "I'm proud of what you do."

Jake tilted her head back and kissed her again. "We have to stop this," he whispered between nibbling kisses. "I can't think when you—oh!"

When they parted again, a great many buttons were undone and their faces were flushed. Jake stroked the creamy base of her throat and undid another button. "I've got three months' vacation owed me and starting right now, I'm taking them. We could have the honeymoon first and then get married whenever you're sure."

Nora glared at him. "I thought we were going to Vegas to get married."

She couldn't believe it when Jake blushed again. He cleared his throat and then looked at her desperately. "I was afraid that was me being an arrogant pig—"

"Skunk," she added meaningfully. "I want to get married in Las Vegas. Last time I let you out of my sight, you disappeared for five months." She bit his earlobe.

"Then, we will. Ouch." Jake disengaged her from him and grinned from ear to ear. "I've been offered a promotion to supervisor, which would mean less field-work. I might take it—I haven't fully decided yet. We can talk about it later."

He nuzzled her throat and then suddenly pulled away. "I haven't heard your answer yet. Nora Stevens, will you marry me?"

"Oh, yes!"

"Good." Jake placed Nora on her feet and reached into his pocket and drew out a postcard of an Egyptian pyramid and threw it on the seat next to him. "Because I'm tired of receiving life-threatening postcards from your matchmakers. We'll invite them to the wedding. That'll get them off my back."

Nora laughed. "Just until they decide we should have children, then they'll probably mail us coupons for baby food."

"Too true," Jake agreed. He looked at her and began to unbutton his shirt.

"Here?" She tried to sound outraged but couldn't disguise her own eagerness.

For an answer Jake kissed her until she forgot where she was—almost.

"Yes." Jake smiled that devilish killer smile. "We need to christen our engagement properly."

And they did.

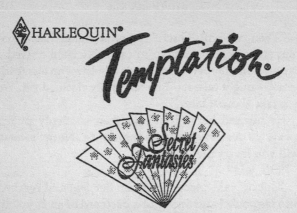

HARLEQUIN®

Temptation.

Secret Fantasies

Do you have a secret fantasy?

Kasey Halliday does—she's fallen hard for the "boy"
next door. Will Eastman is sexy, sophisticated and
definitely interested in Kasey. But there's a mysterious
side to this man she can't quite fathom. Find out what
Will is hiding in #554 STRANGER IN MY ARMS by
Madeline Harper—available in September 1995.

Everybody has a secret fantasy. And you'll find them
all in Temptation's exciting new yearlong miniseries,
Secret Fantasies. Beginning January 1995, one book
each month focuses on the hero's or heroine's
innermost romantic desires....

MILLION DOLLAR SWEEPSTAKES (III)

MOVE OVER, MELROSE PLACE!

As a Privileged Woman, you'll be entitled to all these *Free Benefits.* And *Free Gifts,* too.

To thank you for buying our books, we've designed an exclusive FREE program called *PAGES & PRIVILEGES™*. You can enroll with just one Proof of Purchase, and get the kind of luxuries that, until now, you could only read about.

*B*IG HOTEL DISCOUNTS

A privileged woman stays in the finest hotels. And so can you—at up to 60% off! Imagine standing in a hotel check-in line and watching as the guest in front of you pays $150 for the same room that's only costing you $60. Your *Pages & Privileges* discounts are good at Sheraton, Marriott, Best Western, Hyatt and thousands of other fine hotels all over the U.S., Canada and Europe.

*F*REE DISCOUNT TRAVEL SERVICE

A privileged woman is always jetting to romantic places. When you fly, just make one phone call for the lowest published airfare at time of booking—or double the difference back! PLUS— you'll get a $25 voucher to use the first time you book a flight AND 5% cash back on every ticket you buy thereafter through the travel service!

HT-PP4A

FREE GIFTS!

A privileged woman is always getting wonderful gifts.
Luxuriate in rich fragrances that will stir your senses (and his). This gift-boxed assortment of fine perfumes includes three popular scents, each in a beautiful designer bottle. <u>Truly Lace</u>...This luxurious fragrance unveils your sensuous side. <u>L'Effleur</u>...discover the romance of the Victorian era with this soft floral. <u>Muguet des bois</u>...a single note floral of singular beauty.

YOURS FREE!

$50 VALUE

FREE INSIDER TIPS LETTER

A privileged woman is always informed. And you'll be, too, with our free letter full of fascinating information and sneak previews of upcoming books.

MORE GREAT GIFTS & BENEFITS TO COME

A privileged woman always has a lot to look forward to. And so will you. You get all these wonderful FREE gifts and benefits now with only one purchase...and there are no additional purchases required. However, each additional retail purchase of Harlequin and Silhouette books brings you a step closer to even more great FREE benefits like half-price movie tickets... and even more FREE gifts.

L'Effleur...This basketful of romance lets you discover L'Effleur from head to toe, heart to home.

Truly Lace... A basket spun with the sensuous luxuries of Truly Lace, including Dusting Powder in a reusable satin and lace covered box.

Complete the Enrollment Form in the front of this book and mail it with this Proof of Purchase.

PROOF OF PURCHASE
Offer expires October 31, 1996

HT-PP4